SWORD OF T

BOOK TWO OF THE SO[

Robert Ryan

Cover Design by www.damonza.com

ISBN-13 978-0-9942054-8-3
(print edition)

Trotting Fox Press

Contents

1. Like a Tomb

Gil drew in a breath, but the dust-thickened air choked him. His strength was nearly gone, and hope had faded with it.

Nearby, the earth groaned and more rubble collapsed from the roof of the cave. It sounded like thunder in the confined space. All about him was mayhem. But what disturbed him most were the curses of the Durlin. They were strong men, and fearless, but they were no better off than he was. They were all going to die.

He could not see the Durlin, for the air was a swirling mass of dust that shifted and eddied like the currents of a river. But they were everywhere about him, groping in the dark and calling out.

Though he shielded his eyes from dust and grit with a trembling hand, he still saw nothing through the maelstrom – especially not the daylight at the entrance of the cave that moments ago had served as a signpost of escape. Forced to draw breath again, he coughed and sputtered while his eyes teared up.

But then the horn sounded once more. Hruilgar's horn. The king's huntsman had not deserted them, and though Gil could see nothing he knew from what direction that sound came, and he turned a little to his left and stumbled toward it, for the huntsman had been near the entrance before this chaos had begun. All about him he sensed movement as well. The Durlin were following the sweet sound of hope.

Someone bumped into him. Or he bumped into them. Then he felt a hand on his back, urging him on. He nearly tripped on a fallen rock, but he regained his balance.

When the horn blew again it seemed that it was nearly in his ear, and then he saw the thin frame of Hruilgar and the old man's strong arm quickly reached out and pulled him forward.

There was sudden light, and a breeze on his face. He rushed forward, escaping the cave and then other hands, Durlin hands, were guiding him away from the entrance.

The sun was on his face. The air was fresh once more. He gulped it in and reveled in the relief of escape, in the sensation of open space and freedom.

Behind him the remainder of the Durlin staggered into the light. Taingern was among them, and he began counting men.

"We're all here!" he yelled.

Gil could scarce believe it. They had survived, all of them. His eyes fell on Hruilgar. It was this man who had saved them, but he had not come out unscathed. A rock must have struck him a hard blow, for blood matted the gray hair near his left temple and dripped down his cheek, the red rivulets cutting through the thick layer of grime that coated his face.

There was a noise above him, and Hruilgar looked up.

"Away!" the old man suddenly screamed.

The Durlin reacted instantly. Tired as they were, they wasted no time. The cliff face above the cave entrance began to seethe with treacherous movement, the rock and stone shifting like mud.

They all ran, and Gil ran with them. The earth heaved beneath his feet. The cave entrance seemed to cough and expel dusty air, and then the opening was covered by

4

falling rock. It toppled in a grinding mass, bringing bushes and stunted pines with it. But quick as it began, it ceased just as swiftly.

The Durlin had reached safety some forty paces away, and there they paused. An eerie silence settled over the forest. The ground grew still again. No noise rumbled up from the earth, and the dust in the air silently drifted downward.

Gil looked around. The Durlin were studying the cliff face. Their eyes were grim, but there was a sense of victory in the way they stood. They had survived, and Gil felt it too. Death had been cheated, and life was sweet for all their exhaustion.

He looked at Brand. The regent lay on the ground where the Durlin had carefully placed him. He was conscious, but he seemed very weak. He was not the man that Gil knew, but time and rest would cure that. At least he hoped so.

Gil swore under his breath. Ginsar had a lot to answer for. She was the cause of all this. But the thought of her brought renewed fear. *Where was she?*

Shorty was obviously worried about the same thing. He set a perimeter of guards – the least injured of the Durlin, and they gazed into the shadowy pine forest with alert eyes. Ginsar was out there somewhere, and no matter her assurance of safety for the rest of the day, her promises were like daggers sheathed in an enemy's back.

They rested briefly. Taingern went among them speaking to the men and applying bandages where they were needed and offering words of encouragement. They had all been through much, and seen things beyond their understanding. From time to time their glances strayed to

Brand, but they did not linger long before they shifted uneasily away.

The regent slept. Shorty and Taingern consulted with each other in whispered voices.

Gil sat quietly and thought. He had been taken into the cave by his captors in the late morning. It was now a little after noon. Neither Shorty nor Taingern would like to be here when night fell over the forest. No, they would not risk that. Therefore, the time for rest that they allowed would be short.

Laying back on the grass he closed his eyes and relaxed while he could. He thought of Carnhaina and the quest she had given him. Ginsar had opened a gateway to another world. Forces were loosed upon the land that would tear at reality. She had done this in her madness, in her lust for revenge, and though she thought she could master them they would conquer her instead. So Carnhaina had foretold. And then this world would fall, bit by bit, to the dark forces the sorceress had summoned. Worst of all, Carnhaina had said that *he* must prevent it. That he was born to close the opening that Ginsar had made.

That was all well and good. But she had no idea how he should go about it, and he had even less. It was disturbing to say the least. It was a responsibility that weighed him down. He could not give it to anyone else, but he did not know how to even begin discharging it himself.

"Let's go," Shorty said. His voice was crisp with command and Gil was glad of it. It would be better to be up and moving and to occupy his mind with something else for a while. Getting out of the forest would be the first step – all else could wait.

They began to walk. Shorty did not set a fast pace, for the ground was rough and trees grew thickly the moment they left the clearing. At this rate they would be stuck in the forest overnight. But surely when Brand and the Durlin had come to rescue him they had ridden? Where were the horses?

They went ahead. Soon, Gil realized, they approached the shores of Lake Alithorin. He heard the gentle lap of water and the calls of countless frogs. And then, descending into a concealed gully, he saw the horses and the one Durlin left to guard them. This man asked no questions. His sweeping gaze saw Gil and Brand, measured the state of the Durlin, their dust-covered faces, makeshift bandages and then he immediately began to untie his horse's reins where they were looped around a branch. The other Durlin went for theirs.

When they were all mounted, Brand sitting behind one of the smaller Durlin, Shorty spoke.

"We don't want to be in this forest at night," he said. "So, ride as swiftly as you can down the forest trail. Hruilgar will lead. But ride carefully. Let's go!"

The old huntsman nudged his horse into a trot, and the Durlin followed.

Gil was in their midst. Brand rode a little ahead. The regent sat in the saddle well enough, but he seemed disorientated. Certainly, he was not taking command as Gil knew he would have if he were well. There was something wrong with him, but that was small wonder. For a time, no matter how brief, he had been dead.

They followed Hruilgar back toward Cardoroth. The forest seemed quiet. The gloom amid the trunks grew deeper and the silence heavier as the afternoon wore on. But then, unexpectedly, a wolf howled.

The riders looked about them. The sound did not come again, but their pace quickened and their eyes kept careful watch of the forest.

The afternoon gave way to night. It fell swiftly amid the trees. The silence grew menacing, for now the men expected to hear the wolf again, or the call of others in the pack. But the silence deepened, laying over everything more sinisterly than any howl, and then when there finally was sound again, it was not the wolf at all.

They had come close to the edge of the forest, for the dim light of stars peeked between the thinning canopy, and the trunks of the trees grew further apart. But they were no longer alone. Somewhere ahead was the sound of trotting horses. Then there was a neigh swiftly followed by a muffled curse.

2. Heir to the Throne

The Durlin came to a halt. There was no time to move off the trail, nor any room to spread out in a defensive position. Hruilgar was in the lead, and though not a soldier he drew a long knife. Two Durlin drew their horses level and flanked him; no more would fit on the trail.

Ahead, there was movement. Then riders came into sight. It was a column some twenty strong, and they were armed men, yet they seemed to be surprised to find the Durlin.

The lead rider of the newcomers reined his horse in, coming to a swift stop. The riders behind him did the same.

Gil could not see clearly in the growing dark, but it seemed that they wore the livery of soldiers of Cardoroth. They should be friends, yet there was treachery afoot in the city and these men might owe allegiance to one of the lords who sought to overthrow Brand.

The lead rider was still. Then, slowly, he raised his hand and saluted the Durlin.

"Well met," he said, lowering his hand just as slowly. He was careful to give no indication of reaching for a weapon.

"What are you doing here?" one of the Durlin answered.

The soldier kept his hands still. "We seek the regent, for we have news for him." He hesitated. "We're loyal to him," he added.

Shorty nudged his horse forward and the Durlin on the left eased back to let him through.

"I know you, Drinbar," the Durlindrath said. "Speak freely captain – you're trusted here."

Most of the tension seemed to leave the newcomer, and the men behind him relaxed.

"It's good to see you Shorty. Very good indeed. I have a message for the regent."

The man's eyes flickered toward Brand in the middle of the Durlin.

"Brand is … ill-disposed at the moment," Shorty said.

Drinbar glanced nervously at the regent. "So it seems. I will deliver it to you."

He made to speak again, but Shorty held up his hand. "Brand is ill-disposed, but the heir to the throne is present. Deliver the message to him."

Gil felt the gaze of the captain turn to him, summing him up. He read uncertainty in the man's glance, but Shorty eased his mount back and Gil moved into the space he had left. He did not quite understand what was happening, for Shorty and Taingern were in charge here, but he knew what was expected of him.

"Thank you for coming. You may deliver the message to me."

Drinbar saluted, and his hesitation disappeared.

"Yes, my lord." He gestured back at his men. "We're glad that you've been rescued. But you should know that rumors are abuzz in the city. The nobles have called a council, and they gather from far and wide. Some say Brand is a traitor. Some say he is dead. Some say you're both dead. Frankly, no one knows what's happening. But worse, there are soldiers gathering with the nobles. And they seem to have formed allegiances. To be blunt, the city is in turmoil, and just now anything seems possible."

The man ceased speaking, aware that he may have said too much.

Gil felt everyone's gaze upon him, especially Shorty's and Taingern's. Behind them, Brand dozed in the saddle. This was a situation that Gil had never been in before, and he did not know what he should do. But, he decided to show none of his doubt. Certainly, the two Durlindraths could handle this far better than he could. He knew that. And *they* knew that. This, therefore, was a test for him. They wanted to know what he was made of. Brand was unwell, and someone had to fill the leadership void.

The soldiers ahead of him sat uneasily on their mounts while the silence grew. Gil wondered what Brand would do. Confusion and doubt, he had often said, were the enemy. Correct knowledge and determination, friends.

"Thank you," Gil said, at last knowing what to say. "This has been a time of doubt, but that no longer exists. There is no betrayal. Brand is my friend, and remains regent. He was badly … injured fighting to save me. So, take this message back. Fly with all speed, and we'll follow. Brand is alive. I'm alive. We return to the city, but Cardoroth's enemies gather outside. Plots are afoot, and worse. But Cardoroth, as ever, will endure. And spread the word. Brand remains regent, and I will be king one day, and the nobles who think otherwise are fools. Tell them I said so, and that treachery, schemes and plots against the throne will be punished."

The captain was silent, mulling over those words and measuring the strength of will behind them. A slow smile spread across his face, and then he saluted once more.

"As you wish, my lord! I'll tell them. Personally."

He gave a nod to Shorty and then turned his horse. Giving a command, his men did likewise and they began to gallop back in the direction from whence they came.

Gil noticed that Shorty and Taingern were looking at him.

11

"Well spoken," Shorty said. "But it'll take more than threats to control the nobility if they've really begun to vie for the throne."

Taingern looked at him solemnly. "Do you know what the word was for king in the ancient tongue?"

"No," answered Gil, surprised by the question.

"It was Gorfalac," Taingern informed him.

"What does that mean?"

"It signifies *sword of the blood*, and this you must become. The protector of the realm, the realm's defender."

The moment Gil heard the words, he knew they were true. He looked at Brand. The man had given all that he could, and then more. There would be no further help from him, at least for a while. What was needed now was that Gil himself put to use all that Brand had taught him over the years.

He looked at Brand one final time, but there seemed to be no recognition in the man's eyes.

"Let's go," Gil said.

He nudged his mount forward. His horse responded swiftly. It was Brand's black stallion, and it felt strange to be riding him, but appropriate also.

Gil did not look back, but he knew the others followed. It was but the first step of many that he now must take.

Darkness grew about them. Somewhere behind, the wolf howled again, and there was a sense of loss in that sound, a mournful cry into the heavens that could easily have been human.

It took very little time to reach the eave of the forest. The trees gave way suddenly, the sky opened above, but it was the view ahead that caught Gil's attention.

In the distance was the shadowed mass of Cardoroth. But there were lights within it, flickering and ruddy. There was trouble in Cardoroth as the captain had warned, for the ruddy light was fire. Parts of the city burned. It was worse than the captain had said, but he would not have known. The increasing dark had shown up what was happening better than he would have seen riding into the forest while daylight held.

The captain and his men were somewhere ahead of them on the road, but they had already disappeared into the gloom. Gil hoped they reached the city as soon as possible and spread the word of truth. Both he and Brand were alive. And they were returning. That should give pause to any nobles inciting trouble.

They rode on, slower than the soldiers for they were weary and had many injured men among them. Soon, the scent of smoke drifted to them, and Gil tasted bitterness in his mouth. There were enemies abroad, Ginsar among them, but there were enemies at home too.

3. Like a Rat Down a Hole

They galloped through the rising dark. The smell of smoke grew stronger. There was little talk as they rode, for they were weary and there would be no rest for them when they reached the city. Also, fear was on them, for there was trouble afoot in the kingdom – the kind that led to bloodshed. Already there would have been the flash of swords and the slaying of men. It would get worse swiftly unless order was returned.

Better and better did Gil understand why Shorty had pushed him forward into the role of leader. Leadership was needed now, more than anything, and there were few who could supply it. The role required more than ability; it required the respect of the people. It required a figurehead who could draw the populace together. As prince, that was him. No matter that others, such as Shorty and Taingern, were better skilled. The people would look to him first, as they had done to his forefathers for generations beyond count.

They approached the city, and the great wall of the Cardurleth that surrounded it bulked before them. The fires did not seem so bad as they drew near, or perhaps they were being put out. Gil felt a wave of relief, for if they had begun to spread they would soon reach a point where nothing could stand in their way and the city would be destroyed.

He studied what he could see quite carefully, and it seemed that fires burned now in isolated spots. Even those were rapidly diminishing. The populace must have worked well and swiftly to control them. For all the betrayal and treachery in the city, most of the people were fiercely proud and loyal. They loved their home and they fought for it.

The West Gate came into view, the Arach Neben in the old tongue. The road was white beneath the hooves of the horses, gleaming pale beneath the stars. The wall, though pockmarked by the ravages of war, seemed smooth and graceful in the dim light.

Gil shuddered. It was here that he had first seen the Rider called Death. It was not a good memory. Brand had walked through the gate to face him, but the gate was now closed and the ornament of the Morning Star that decorated it shone fitfully.

The riders drew up. Soldiers moved behind the thick gate-bars.

"Who comes to Cardoroth?" asked one of the soldiers, his figure dim and his voice sounding hollow in the gate-tunnel.

Gil paused a moment. He did not know for certain where the loyalty of these men lay, but he had the Durlin with him. Also, this was the very gate where Brand himself had once been a captain. The men knew him well.

He edged his mount forward. "Open, for I am Gil, Prince of Cardoroth, and the regent and the Durlin are with me."

There was a pause while the shadowy figure peered through the gate. Then there was a rough command and several men moved swiftly.

The gate swung open. A flickering torch was lit, and by its light Gil saw the present-day captain standing there with several men behind him.

The captain saluted, his gaze taking in the tattered Durlin and the quiet figure of Brand.

Gil returned the salute. "At ease, captain."

The man relaxed. "We're glad to see you. And Brand too." He seemed genuine, and Gil guessed that this was one of the men who had personally served under Brand in the past.

"What's been happening here?" Gil asked.

"We're not quite sure. We know there has been some fighting, and trouble among the nobles. But the fires are nearly out now and the city has grown quiet. I sent a man in to find out what was happening, but he hasn't returned yet."

Gil thought about that. But not for long. There was no way to know what was happening, but Brand had taught him never to show indecision. He did not know for sure what was going on in the city, yet there were only two ways to find out. Wait here until word reached him, or enter and find out for himself.

"Thank you, captain. We'll go through now."

The captain moved aside, and his men followed. They all gave a salute, but it was for Brand rather than Gil. But the regent sat slumped in his saddle, and there were concerned looks in the eyes of the soldiers as the Durlin rode past.

They entered the dark gate-tunnel. The clatter of hooves was loud. The confined space here always made Gil nervous, but it was worse now. It was a killing ground, and many were the slots in the wall from which arrows could be loosed.

He rode ahead. The Durlin rode with him. In moments, the tunnel gave way to a city street and the star-strewn heavens opened above.

"Where to?" Shorty asked.

"The palace," Gil said without hesitation.

They pressed forward, riding close and keeping their eyes open. At first, it was quiet, but as they turned a corner there were suddenly people on the street. They saw Gil and Brand, and recognized them swiftly.

The Durlin bunched closer, but there was no need to worry. A cheer went up from several in the crowd, and then they all joined in.

Suddenly there were more people. They saw Brand and the cheer grew into a chant.

Brand! Brand! Brand!

Gil felt a surge of pride. He looked at the regent, and Brand seemed to rally, sitting straighter in the saddle and looking around. He offered a little wave to the crowd, and the chanting swelled louder.

Taingern whispered in Gil's ear. "Brand always says he isn't well liked in Cardoroth, but he's been dealing with the nobles too long. The people love him."

Gil knew it was true.

They rode on, heading toward the palace. The scent of smoke was pungent in the air, but there were no fires to be seen, nor any burned buildings. Not on the main road at least.

They entered the palace grounds. Taingern and Shorty flanked him protectively now.

"There," Shorty said, nodding curtly to the left.

Gil looked in the direction that Shorty had indicated, but saw nothing.

"Look at the grass," Taingern instructed.

Gil saw it then. There were scuffle marks and bare earth had been exposed. Something glistened darkly too.

"Blood," Shorty confirmed.

They moved through the gardens slowly. There were more signs of fighting, and Gil sensed the Durlin growing tense all about him.

There was movement ahead near the palace doors. Someone rushed out, but Gil saw that it was Arell.

The healer moved swiftly. And there was fear on her face too. Gil knew then that the rumors were true: she was Brand's lover.

There was concern etched into her expression, and she had eyes only for Brand. Yet as she neared she looked at Gil also, and he saw her relief. But she went straight to the regent.

"Brand? Brand?" she said.

The regent looked at her, but gave no answer.

Arell's face was white, but she seemed professional and in control. She assisted while a Durlin helped Brand dismount, and then at Taingern's nod several Durlin dismounted and took the regent toward the chambers of healing. Arell supported him on one side, but he walked at a slow pace as though he were a man half asleep.

The rest of them dismounted also, and the remainder of the Durlin led the horses toward the stables. Shorty and Taingern stayed with Gil.

"Is it safe, do you think?"

"Of course," Shorty answered. "Otherwise Arell would have said something."

Gil cursed inwardly. He should have reasoned that through himself.

They entered the palace. There were soldiers on guard everywhere. They looked at Gil. Most glanced away quickly, but some few showed surprise. He guessed that word of his capture had spread wide, and that there were rumors of his death.

But he was not dead, nor was Brand. Somehow, they had survived an encounter with Death. But not without scars. Gil began to wonder if Brand would ever be the same man again.

"Where should we go first?" Gil asked.

"The throne room," Shorty answered. "There we'll find some answers to what's been going on in our absence."

"But what if nobody is there?"

Shorty shrugged. "Then we'll send for them. But this is an emergency. And word of our return will have come before us. Someone will be there."

"But why the throne room?"

"Because that's where orders are most often given from. It's a place of authority, and in an emergency people seek that out."

They walked through the corridors. For all that Shorty said it was safe, he and Taingern proceeded with care, their hands never far from their sword hilts and their eyes alert for any sign of danger.

It did not take long to reach the throne room. Soldiers stood without, and Gil saw tension ease from his two companions. These were men that they obviously knew and trusted.

The soldiers opened the great doors. Gil walked through with the Durlindraths. The marble floor was white and polished, and their steps echoed loudly around the room. It was especially the vaulted ceiling far above that cast the sound back and made it sound as though there were double the number of people.

An older lady was there; one whom Gil was sure that he had seen before, and yet not one that he knew.

The lady was by herself, but she seemed at ease. Moreover, neither Shorty nor Taingern seemed surprised. Gil began to wonder exactly who she was.

"It's good to see you," she said, addressing both the Durlindraths. Her eyes strayed momentarily to Gil, and he felt the keen intelligence of her mind, weighing him up and forming opinions swiftly. He was not sure he liked it, but he had the feeling that most of her judgements, whatever they were, were likely proved correct by time.

He saw an unspoken question pass between Shorty and the woman. Whatever it was, Shorty seemed to have received an answer, for he turned to Gil and spoke.

"I have the honor," he said, in a voice somewhat more formal than usual, "to introduce you to Esanda. She has no title, is not of the nobility, and yet she served in the highest capacity as a counselor to your grandfather and now, in turn, to Brand."

The old lady inclined her head ever so slightly. Gil studied her, and was amazed. He knew all the counselors. Every one of them. She was not among them. So, who was she?

"Pleased to meet you, madam," he said. If he was surprised and confused, he was not going to show it.

Esanda laughed. "Ah, Brand has taught you well indeed. You do not have a clue who I am, although I know you very well. But you refuse to be thrown off balance. Nor do you even ask who I am, and why I am not known at court."

Gil was beginning to get an idea, and random comments and bits of information that had previously seemed unconnected to fell into place.

"Brand has taught me well, but I fear I'm not a great student. Nevertheless, I can make some deductions."

"And what do you deduct?"

"Only this. If your presence and identity have been kept a secret, it is for a purpose. What purpose could that be? Well, one where the work you do can best be achieved anonymously. What work lends itself to this situation? I can only think of one answer. Madam, you are a spy. More than that, given that you advised my grandfather and now the regent, I should say you are *the* spy. There would be a network of them, but you are at its head, the holder of every secret in the realm. Even," he added with a rueful smile, "the ones a mischievous prince would prefer to have kept to himself."

Taingern chuckled. Shorty winked at him, but Esanda studied him with a long and appraising glance before she smiled.

"I'm impressed. Brand has indeed taught you well. There's a beauty in logic, and that was a masterpiece of sound reasoning. Moreover, everything you say is right." She paused. "It's pleasing to know that I don't work for dolts. That being the case, I don't need to warn you that you must keep your ... guesses to yourself."

"Of course," Gil answered promptly. He understood that he had been entrusted with a state secret, and no force on earth would ever get him to utter a word of what he knew.

"Good. Now, we had better get down to business, and swiftly. Much is afoot."

Gil listened as she spoke. He remembered her now, a shadowy presence throughout his life, somehow always around but seldom ever seen.

She gave details of what had happened while they were out of the city.

"Dernbrael called a Council of Nobles as he had threatened to do. But it did not work out quite as he expected. There was much talk, and much talk against Brand. But for all of that, there were not that many who wanted to move openly against him."

Shorty grunted. "A bunch of cowards," he said. "Soft to the core like a rotten apple."

"True," Esanda agreed. "But there are some who are loyal to Brand. But more still fear him. Between that, and the fact that many of the noble houses think they may yet have a chance at the throne, Dernbrael did not get the support he anticipated."

"He probably didn't bribe them enough," Taingern said.

"That too," Esanda agreed. "Dernbrael has expensive tastes in many things, and a fondness for betting on slow horses as well. His wealth is greatly reduced these last few years, and that may also be spurring him along the course he's chosen. As king, he would find a way to redistribute treasury funds into his own name."

"But surely," Taingern said, "he didn't attempt to have himself crowned straightaway? He would seek the regency first, would he not?"

"His financial position may have driven him further than was wise," Esanda told them. "He went for the highest prize, grasped at it with both hands."

"And what happened?" asked Gil.

"He failed," Shorty said. "Or else we would have all been arrested when we returned."

Esanda gave a solemn nod. "Shorty is right. He failed. The vote went against him, because he tried to force the issue too soon. The nobles were not ready for that decision, not at all. Especially when Brand might still be alive, when he might return and make them regret it."

"Is he regent then?" asked Taingern. "But that cannot be, or we would still have been arrested."

Esanda grinned. "The man is a fool. He risked too much, pushed too hard for the crown, and that caused great divisiveness. When it failed, that mistrust and divisiveness remained. He lost the vote to be regent as well. One that he might otherwise have won."

"And the fires we saw in the city?" Gil asked. "How did that happen? Dernbrael must have been desperate."

"Ah, you see where this is going. Yes, he was desperate, for he saw the chance of a lifetime slipping between his fingers. He tried to force the issue, just him and the factions most closely aligned to him. He tried to take the palace, thinking that once he had that, and that once Brand was dead or discredited, he could rouse the people to support him, and at that point a vote of the council was redundant."

"But the soldiers stationed in the palace fought him off," stated Shorty.

"Indeed. He underestimated their loyalty to Brand. He came with a force of over a hundred, but it wasn't enough."

"And where is he now?" Gil asked.

"He's in hiding. Disappeared like smoke on the wind," Esanda answered.

Shorty clenched his fists. "More like a rat down a hole."

Esanda grinned at him. "Yes, that too. But there are only so many rat holes in Cardoroth, and sooner or later I'll find the one he's using."

Gil did not doubt this was true. One way or another, sooner or later, Dernbrael would show up. But that was a problem for another day. What to do now? That was the question. And as soon as he asked it of himself, he realized that the others had grown quiet. They were asking themselves the same thing.

He looked around at them. Their eyes were all upon him. And he knew that they were weighing him, scrutinizing him. Esanda's gaze was the sharpest of them all, but they must all have been wondering the same thing in their own ways.

They looked at him because he was the future of Cardoroth, if it were to have one. Only he could unite the people. It was his destiny, his responsibility. And right there in that moment he understood what leadership was. A king, a leader of any kind, served those he led. He did what he did for them, and them alone, rather than himself. He did it because it was right, and because it was his duty. Not because he wanted to.

Gil sighed. It seemed that he must sacrifice his dream of learning deeply about magic. When he spoke though, he was decisive and there was no regret in his voice.

"Right then," he said to Esanda. "I would like you to find Dernbrael. No matter what hole he has gone down, I would speak with him. I would tell him what I think of his treachery, for I am heir to the throne. Then I would see him brought to justice. There can be no tolerance of treason, not when the realm is at risk. And his capture and punishment will send a message to the other nobles. Their chance has passed. Whatever opportunity they had is gone. I *will* be king, whether I want it or not, whether *they* want it or not. I would willingly renounce my claim to the throne for Brand. I would follow him all the days of my life, but it's clear that he's unwell, and if he recovers I don't think he'll stay in Cardoroth much longer. He too has a destiny … and it calls him. Just as does mine."

He felt their gazes on him again. They were weighing him and judging him anew. And this time there was growing approval in their expressions.

4. Anticipate the Enemy

There was a glitter in Esanda's eyes.

"Truly, Brand has taught you well. But I see your grandparents in you also." She stood. "I'll work on it. Dernbrael will be found. Someone, somewhere, knows where he is. I hear every whisper in the city, eventually. Word will come to me. More importantly, we have a leader that the people of Cardoroth can follow." She gave him a slight bow and left the room.

Gil turned to Shorty. "How is Brand? You've known him longest … is he going to be alright?"

Shorty shook his head. "It's impossible to say, lad. There's something wrong, that's for sure. He's not as he was, or as he would want to be."

"No, he is not," Taingern said. "But we must have faith in Carnhaina. She would not have brought him back from death itself only for him to die soon after or fail to regain his strength."

"I think you're right," Gil agreed. "But what man could go through what Brand has and not be unchanged? Even damaged?"

"Brand is not as other men," Shorty said softly.

Gil agreed with that. But still, he remembered what he had seen on that mountain somewhere in the spirit world when Brand had died.

Carnhaina had spoken to the regent, but Gil had not heard the words. He wished he knew what they were. Brand had answered, and there was a look on his face that

Gil could not begin to understand. Then Brand had lifted high his arms and looked to the sky. The mountain on which they stood lurched. The queen pointed at him with her spear, and lightning flashed from the heavens. It struck the regent, searing him, running the length of his body. But he stood still and kept his arms up as though to embrace it. Thrice the lightning struck. And the last was a searing bolt that sizzled through the air, struck him, and leaped to the stone near his feet. The rock had split. Water gushed through the crack and hastened in a stream down the slope and into the valley. What had it all meant? Was any of it even real, or was it in their minds? But there was magic at work, mighty magic, for back in the chamber where Brand lay dead his chest heaved, and then with a great gasp he gulped in life-giving air.

Gil would never forget what he had seen. Brand would be changed, but Gil must put all that aside for now. He must think of the next step, of what was best for Cardoroth, as Brand would have wanted him to do. He must anticipate the enemy.

Gil considered the situation. There were two enemies. The first was internal, part of Cardoroth itself. The nobles were among that group, but they were not the only ones. There were dark forces within the city too. Forces in allegiance with Cardoroth's enemies.

For the moment, he could do nothing about Dernbrael. He trusted that Esanda would find him, and Gil guessed that the noble was not only in hiding, but in fear of his life. His plan had failed, and both Gil and Brand had returned to the city alive. Dernbrael would be desperate, but that also made him dangerous. Could he do anything besides hide? Had he any last strategies available to him?

26

Gil's thoughts shifted to the external enemies of Cardoroth. What would they do? What of the quest that Carnhaina had given him that would defeat them?

She had revealed that Ginsar had loosed forces upon the land that tore at reality. In her madness, in her lust for revenge against Brand, she opened a gateway and drew them in. Carnhaina had warned that however much she strove to master them, they would conquer her instead. And after, they would turn upon the world to make it all their own. How earnest Carnhaina had seemed! There was almost fear in her voice, and she had charged Gil with preventing that catastrophe. She had charged him with closing the gateway that Ginsar had made. But when he asked her how, she had said that she did not know, that he must discover for himself. But that it was for this that he had been born.

It all seemed too much. There were too many enemies, too many things that he did not know.

He turned to Shorty and Taingern. "How are we going to do this? Where should I even start?"

5. A Son of my Sons

Gil knew that the quest was what mattered most. Carnhaina's charge must be his priority, for if the forces of which she warned were unleashed upon Alithoras the entire land would be destroyed. Dernbrael was nothing compared to that. And yet, could he be sure there was no connection between them? It was possible that Ginsar was a link between them all, the single thread sewn through an entire tapestry.

One thing he knew for sure. He could not do everything at once, nor all by himself. He must delegate.

"Shorty, Taingern … listen to me." He spoke with resolve. "You know that I'm not yet ready to be king. I'm still young. But Brand is ill, and I have to step up to my responsibilities. The kingdom must have a leader who can unify. Brand did it, because, well, he's Brand. Now, as heir, it must be me. But I'll need your help."

"Lad," Shorty said. "You have it."

Taingern looked him in the eye. "Lord, we are at your service."

Gil felt a surge of loyalty wash over him. These were true men. Handpicked by Brand, and each of them had survived terrible dangers with their leader. They were men of courage and men of reliability. They were also smart men, and as Brand had often told him, it did not matter a whit that they were as chalk and cheese. When it mattered, they would both do the same thing: give their all.

"Right," Gil said. "Ginsar has opened a way between worlds and allowed these dangerous forces into Alithoras. Carnhaina has charged me with closing that gateway, with sending those forces back whence they came. I must concentrate on that. No one else in Cardoroth has any understanding of the magic as do I. I shall send word to Lòrenta and seek help from the lòhrens, but I fear that the problem will need solving before any help from that quarter can arrive."

"And what of Dernbrael?" Shorty asked.

"I have a feeling that Esanda always finds whatever she searches for. He'll turn up, and I can wait until then. In the meantime, we'll forget him." Gil had a thought while he spoke. "We could, of course, brand him as a traitor and issue orders for his arrest. But that will only send him deeper into hiding. Better to stay silent. Let him think that just maybe he might not be a priority. He may get careless then and give Esanda a better chance to discover him."

"And what of the nobles who sided with him?"

Gil thought about that. "There was nothing improper in the Council of Nobles itself, and they were free to cast their vote there and express opinions. Forget about them. But the nobles who gathered force afterward, who assisted Dernbrael to assault the palace, that is a different matter. That was treason, and more. The whole city could have burned. Get the City Watch onto them. Have them arrested, and held in prison. There need not be any trial until after the crisis with Ginsar is averted."

Shorty chuckled. "The captain of the City Watch was appointed by Brand. He was not a noble, and they will not like being arrested by him, not one bit."

"I think I can live with their discomfit," Gil said. "Oh, and that being the case, please tell the captain to arrest them in public places. That'll help spread word that treason isn't tolerated."

"More than that," Taingern added, "the people will like it that one of their own is arresting the nobles."

"Excellent," Gil said. "What else should we do?"

"I suggest increasing the guard around the palace," Shorty said. "The Durlin are tired, and we cannot be sure there won't be another attempt on your life."

"Agreed. And send out scouts into the wild as well. Cardoroth's enemies may attack after recent events, sensing turmoil in the city."

Shorty scratched his head. "I think that might be about it, at least for the moment."

"Not quite," Gil answered. "There's one thing more, but I must do it myself. Still, it's best that you know about it."

The two Durlindraths looked at him with interest.

"Carnhaina told me that she didn't know how the gateway between worlds could be closed. But I must discover it as she charged me to do, and I've been thinking."

He felt a wave of determination rise within him. He thought of what Brand had given for Cardoroth. He thought of his grandparents. They had never given up, even in the darkest of hours. He knew there would be a way to do what he must, and he would keep seeking until he found it. But there was a place to start.

"There's a secret chamber behind Brand's bedroom. It was built long ago, by Carnhaina herself. She used it as a library, or a study. I think it was a place where she would not be disturbed when she practiced magic."

He felt the eyes of the two men on him. They were listening carefully, wondering where this was going.

"In that room I've found a diary. At least, it's mostly a diary, but at times she addresses me directly."

Taingern raised an eyebrow. "Are you sure? She died long, long ago. It was another age."

"I'm sure," Gil said without hesitation. "It's hard to know just what her powers were, but certainly one of them was foresight. And that might be a good choice of words, for though I can give no rational explanation for it, that's where I feel I must start my quest. There'll be something there, some snippet of information."

Even as he spoke, he felt the truth of those words in his bones. It was not something that he had felt before, but Brand had spoken of it. For a warrior or for a lòhren, instincts often prompted action.

"Sounds to me like a good place to start," Shorty said.

"The reason I'm telling you," Gil explained, "is that I'm not sure how long it'll take. The diary is large and sometimes hard to understand. I could be there for many hours at a time, and I wouldn't like you to think that I'm shirking my responsibilities."

Taingern clapped him on the shoulder. "Don't be concerned. We know you take this seriously. Gil, you're no longer a child, and we know it. Do what you must do, and follow your instincts. Brand was always at his best when he was like that."

"And we'll send some Durlin with you," Shorty added. "You must go nowhere without them now."

Gil thought how much had changed in such a short period. Only days ago the thought of a guard chafed at him. Now, he wanted nothing more. This was going to be a dangerous period, and he longed for Brand to get well and take over. But that might never happen. Anyway, he was close to manhood now, and he knew better than to

31

wish for things. He must make them happen if he wanted them to happen at all. And all else he must accept with good grace.

They went to the great doors and Shorty opened them. Two Durlin waited without. They had changed their clothes and washed. The white surcoats that they wore, markers of their position as Durlin, gleamed. Gil felt dirty and wanted a wash and a change of clothes as well, but that could wait.

He left Shorty and Taingern then, moving up through the palace to higher floors. The Durlin walked with him, silent and watchful. He did not mind their presence; he was in fact reassured by it, and he cursed himself for being a foolish boy all those times they annoyed him in the past.

The Durlin walked a pace behind him most of the way. They seldom spoke, keeping their eyes and ears alert to their surroundings. This behavior was only changed when they approached a corner. At such a time, one Durlin went ahead first while the other stepped up to be level with Gil.

They reached Brand's room. The door was closed, but Gil knew that Brand was not there. Arell was caring for him down below in the chambers of healing.

He knocked on the door just to be sure, but there was no answer. Then one of the Durlin opened it and went through, Gil following.

The room was clean and tidy, and the bed was made. Suddenly, Gil felt loss wash over him. Brand may never be well enough to live life as he had done again. Perhaps he would be confined to the chambers of healing for the rest of his life. If so, it was Gil's fault. Or maybe not directly his fault, but something for which he knew he would always feel guilty. Not quite the same thing, but not a good feeling either.

He walked to the far wall. There he hesitated before turning back to the Durlin. "Don't be alarmed," he said. "And please, keep to yourself what you're about to see."

"Of course," one of them answered in a steady voice. But he could tell they did not like it. Their hands strayed to the hilts of their swords.

Gil held his right palm to the wall. Straightaway the sign of Halathgar, the two pale dots like eyes, began to tingle. Then he invoked lòhrengai. He felt it spring to life, stronger, more sure than it ever had before. Something had happened in his struggle with Ginsar, something had been woken inside him.

Light glimmered on his palm. He did not think too deeply about it, but just accepted that it had come at his need, just as he knew it always would.

"Halathgar!" he commanded.

Light flared, a dazzling blue that filled the chamber. He felt a power respond to his own. It rose up, sought him out, assessed him and recognized who he was. Then, satisfied, it withdrew. As it did so, stone ground on stone and a door appeared.

Gil lowered his hand. The blue light faded. He turned once more to the Durlin. He saw now that their hands gripped their sword hilts, but they still appeared calm.

He thought for a moment. "Best that you stay here," he said. "I'm safe in the room beyond."

"We should go with you everywhere," one of them replied.

"Not here, I think," Gil answered. "This was once the study of Carnhaina. It's small, and you will find it uncomfortable. Stay in this room and relax. I won't be more than an hour or so."

He stepped through the door. "Halathgar," he said once more, and the door slid closed with a grumble behind him.

He breathed in of the air. It smelled of secrets, of long-forgotten magic. But it was dim, and he summoned light to his hand and then, without thinking, cast it gently upward. It floated to the ceiling and stayed there. It was a strange light, bright and warm, but it had a shiver like starlight to it. Stranger still was that Brand had not taught him how to do that. But he had said that the magic had a life of its own, and that when it began to flow through him it would express itself in different ways from what Brand could do or teach. *None of us is the same, nor the magic we wield. Learn what you can do. Test yourself. You are the magic and the magic is you.*

He looked about the room. It was lavish though small, if somewhat long and narrow. A couch, lush and soft, filled most of it. Dust covered it now, but the color of the fabric shone through. Royal blue.

The hangings on the wall were the same color, and Gil studied them, breathing in their history, the history of his ancestors. The tent camps and villages by a great river. Beyond, the forest. And within the deeps of the trees a mighty city. Halathar, the home of the immortals who had befriended and taught many tribes of men. There were more images. One showed the legendary standing stones, a place of ceremony that dated back to his earliest ancestors. It was a place from history that was not forgotten, but that had become myth. It was part of the *Age of Heroes.*

Then he saw the migration of the Camar tribes as they traveled eastward. But there was war also. Massive battles against the enemies from the south were shown. There were elugs, which some called goblins, and their mighty armies were so vast as to darken the wall-hangings. Elùgroths commanded them, cloaked in shadow and pointing wych-wood staffs with the menace of sorcery.

Gil loved it all. It was the memory of another time, of an age before his. But the more things changed, the more they stayed the same. All this could come to pass again. Would come to pass, unless he fulfilled Carnhaina's charge.

His glance turned to the desk, and the book set upon it. Why was he drawn to this? Was it magic? Was it destiny? Why should he think there were any answers there for him? Then again, why would there not be? This was his connection to Carnhaina, to his great ancestor, and somewhere in his heritage was sure to lie the answers he sought. Why else would Ginsar wish him dead?

He sat down and opened the book at random. One place was as good as another to read, but he wished that Elrika was here as she had been last time. It was not the same without her. He missed her, and he had much to tell her. She was really the only person he could confide in, or *wanted* to confide in. Brand was like a father to him. Shorty and Taingern like uncles. But she was different. She was something else…

But the book called to him, and he began to read. He flicked through pages, waiting for something to trigger his instincts.

"Evil," Carnhaina wrote at one point. "What is it? Men call it Dark, and themselves Light. But does not a bright Light cause blindness? And does not the Dark offer nurture and comfort? Are each of these elements also not a part of man? Certainly, he is made of both, for all men and woman carry the seeds of each within them. Perhaps

35

evil is a term for those who do not struggle. To give in to the Dark entirely might be evil. But evil sees it as a purity of spirit, as a person fulfilling their destiny. Am I evil because I understand the Dark? Some say that I am. Fools. I am neither Light nor Dark. I am Carnhaina, and that is enough for me."

Gil read, trying to grapple with the issues. He knew that Cardoroth's philosophers wrestled with them too. And they had answers, which he did not. Did that make them smarter than him? Or were they fools, thinking to unravel the secrets of humanity and understand the hearts of men, thinking they understood and all the while oblivious to their ignorance?

"Elùdrath!" Carnhaina wrote, and Gil sensed her enmity leap off the page. "He is evil, beyond doubt. Or at least my enemy, which is the same thing. It is from him that the Dark in this land spreads. He is its center, its origin. The Dark Lord! The Shadowed Lord! The master of elùgroths. To combat him the Halathrin ventured to this land, made their exodus leaving behind all that they knew in exchange for struggle and woe. Ah! A great people, but they have their flaws too. Who does not?"

Gil felt that he was reading history, as he was, but he was also in Carnhaina's mind. These were her words, her thoughts, her innermost musings.

"Shurilgar! May a thousand fires burn out his eyes. The Betrayer of Nations. His Darkness is strong, strong! And yet he is but a servant of Elùdrath. The wicked are mighty, but the Light has power too. But men? Most are fools. They forget. They fail to think. Shurilgar will come to a bad end, I can see that now, but it will not be by my hand. Elùdrath is different. He is beyond my sight. Men think him dead. But I feel in my bones it is not so. He lives! And his darkness will spread through the long ages to come."

The words sent a shiver up Gil's spine. Brand had once whispered something to him, something like that. *Why do the elugs attack us? Who controls them, drives their enmity?*

He turned the page, and then turned some more. Something stood out to him. The script was different, as though Carnhaina was older.

"In time, a son of my son's distant sons will be borne. Power shall be his. He will be marked with the sign of Halathgar. Evil will overshadow the land, and four Riders shall come, and death and destruction will be as their shadow, following in their wake wherever they go. Behold! The void shall be breached, for the Riders come not of this world. The gateways will open. The possible will be impossible. The impossible possible. But harken to my words – the powers that form and substance the world will seek balance. If evil is born, so too is good. It shall rise amid the shadows. Look for it. Seek it out. Revere it, for it is the key…"

The text cut off there, but there was a drawing. It was by Carnhaina's hand, and the image was of her tower, of the Tower of Halathgar. There was a trapdoor, and then a stairway leading underground. Gil remembered seeing that trapdoor. But what lay beneath it? The drawing did not say. The stairs petered out and at their end were two twinkling dots, like stars. It was the Seal of Halathgar. That was all. Was it a hint of something? But that did not make sense. Stars did not shine underground. Was the drawing even connected to the text? There seemed no connection between them at all, but the drawing *did* appear straight after it.

He flicked through some more pages, but there was nothing else that stood out to him. The next sections were about the administration of a kingdom. What taxes were raised, what effect they had on employment and how to balance the need to raise state revenue with the necessity of stimulating the economy.

Gil put the diary down. He began to have the feeling that this was not an ordinary book. It called to him to read it, but he was not sure if the pages were the same each time he picked it up. And as though it knew when he had read what he was intended to, it showed him boring material that discouraged him from reading more.

He leaned back in the chair. Perhaps he had read enough anyway, but whether that was the book or his own instinct, he was not so sure. His curiosity was raised though. He allowed his feelings to rise, to replace his rational thought. He did not seek an answer, did not ask himself any questions. He just let his feelings flow unchecked through him.

This was a meditation that Brand had taught him. He saw again the image of the tower, and his feelings swirled and surged. He acknowledged them but viewed them dispassionately, as though they belonged to someone else. What dominated? Unbidden, the answer came to him. Curiosity. He must go back to the Tower of Halathgar and discover what was beneath the trapdoor. Fear was entwined with curiosity though. He knew he might learn more there, and the magic within him stirred in response. He felt that it was right to return, but that it might come with some cost. There may be danger. Yes, there was definitely danger, but then cold fear shot through him. Was the danger ahead of him, or was it present now? His emotions surged again, and he began to think with the rational part of his mind.

The dispassionate feeling evaporated, and he lost the feel of the meditation. With a long breath he stood up. It was time to go. He took one last look at the room, knowing he would return here again and again. Then he invoked the magic and opened the door into Brand's room. Stepping through, he closed it behind him.

Straightaway, he sensed that something was wrong.

6. A Duthenor Warrior

Gil studied the room. He saw nothing that should not have been there. It was lavish, so unlike Brand, and yet it was the bedroom of kings and queens back into antiquity. Brand would have had little choice in the furnishings or historical decorations. They probably remained much the same generation after generation.

His gaze swept over it all. The bed was made, the rugs on the floor clean. Two cushions rested neatly on the couch, and there was no dust anywhere. The weapons that hung on the wall glittered. Even the dark walnut bookshelf was polished to a smooth shine. That at least was a personal mark Brand had made on the room: he loved to read.

Gil went still. He knew what was wrong. The Durlin were not there. They would not have left this place, not even for a moment. Unless, of course, they had merely decided to wait outside the regent's personal quarters.

The door to the corridor was closed. Did the Durlin close it after they entered the bedroom? He could not remember. And if they had gone out, why had they not left it open?

He stood motionless, and listened. He heard nothing. Quickly, he summoned the magic within him. With it he could detect if there were people outside the door, perhaps even recognize if they were the Durlin. He was about to cast it forth with his hands when sudden movement disturbed him.

Out from behind the couch leapt a man. It was not one of the Durlin. He moved quickly, a dagger in his hand, and his strides were swift and purposeful.

Assassin. The word rang like a bell in Gil's mind. But it was not the same man who had attacked him before. And beyond doubt this one intended to kill him. He saw determination glitter in the intruder's pale eyes.

The assassin lunged toward him. Gil lifted high his hands. He had not yet discovered how to summon lòhrenfire, the weapon of choice for lòhrens, but nevertheless a bright light flashed from his palms blinding the man.

Gil stepped to the side. He darted to the wall and drew a blade. If he had not already had the magic summoned, he would be dead. But now the magic was alive within him, and he held a blade of cold steel in his hand. It was a chance at life, and he was going to make the most of it.

The assassin hesitated, perhaps still blinded though more likely confused. Few knew that Gil studied the arts of a lòhren. Gil stepped forward, intending to take advantage of the situation. But the man reacted swifter than expected.

In a smooth and practiced motion, he hurled his dagger. Gil twisted to the side, but still the blade tore at his shoulder. Pain flared.

There was no hesitation now. The man drew his sword and advanced. He lunged forward in a killing blow. Gil stepped back, using his own blade to deflect the strike. He followed through with a riposte, his sword flicking deftly at his attacker's neck, but the man was too skilled to succumb. He deflected the counterattack with ease and then drove forward in a flurry of swift and deadly strikes.

Gil held his own. The man was skilled, perhaps more skilled than he was. But there was fear on him, and it caused him to hurry. If he were caught, he would be sentenced to death. So he attacked with all he had. Gil, on the other hand, realized he need only defend. Time was in his favor. He could call for help, but there was a pride in him that refused to do that. Besides, the clang of blade on blade would soon be heard by someone.

He defended, being sure not to allow himself to be cornered. He tried to maneuver toward the door, but the attacker would have none of that.

"Die, you bastard!" the man said with intense force.

It was an eerie feeling for Gil to hear those words, to know that someone wished him dead with all his heart. And yet it gave him strength too. This man was becoming frustrated, and that meant Gil was doing well.

They moved to the other side of the room, past the bed. Blades flicked and ragged breaths were drawn. Gil realized something else. The man had spoken with an accent. He sounded like Brand, only his accent was far stronger. Brand, as he mastered all other things to which he turned his attention, had learned the dialect of Cardoroth to near-perfection. This man had not.

Gil felt the magic within him grow restless. It was time to use it again, to see if he could once more surprise his attacker.

They moved toward the couch, and the assassin's desperation grew. He had counted on a quick killing, not a drawn-out fight. Gil grinned at him, seeking to unbalance him, but the Duthenor was a professional. He merely pressed his attack forward just as he had been doing.

Gil saw something on the floor, and his grin vanished. There was a pool of blood, dark red and stark. It splashed across a beautifully-woven rug.

42

Then he saw the body. Horror washed over him. It was of a Durlin, and an arrow protruded from the back of his neck. But the assassin carried no bow … and Gil suddenly realized that the man had an accomplice. He would be outside, keeping guard so that the assassin remained undisturbed. But they would not have expected their quarry to disappear: they knew nothing of the secret library. How long had they been waiting? And where was the second Durlin? And what was to stop the accomplice from entering now to aid his comrade?

7. Cold as Ice

The attacker must have sensed uncertainty. Gil had been thrown off balance by the sight of the dead Durlin, and then by the realization that there were *two* assassins. The intruder came at him again in a desperate rush. Time was running out.

Steel clanged against steel, and gone was all pursuit of skill. This was an attack of brute strength, driven by cold fury and desperation, but still controlled by a professional warrior who did not panic.

Gil could not stand his ground. He gave way, yet he did so grudgingly, step by step, deflecting his opponent's powerful strikes rather than blocking them.

He saw the desperation of the man grow, and his confidence increased accordingly. Brand had taught him well. He had survived all that this warrior, this assassin, could throw at him, and he was still there. Young as he was, he had skill enough to withstand his enemy, and for the first time he believed that not only could he fend him off, but that he could defeat him.

The fear that had sunk into Gil's belly at the beginning of the fight was less now. And anger stirred. This man had killed a Durlin, was trying to kill him. He had endured enough of that lately. No more.

Gil slowed his retreat. The attacker, wearied by his onslaught, could no longer strike as swiftly or as powerfully as he had been doing. One moment he had dominated the fight, and the next the situation was reversed.

With dazzling speed Gil unleashed his own attack. He was mad, anger burning hotter and hotter within him, but he ignored it as Brand had trained him to do. He just let his skill take over, allowed his arms and body to move with freedom, allowed them to flow with the grace and deadliness of the techniques that he had long practiced.

The assassin stumbled. Glad was Gil then for Brand's training, for the anger within him rose up and sought to leap forward with a killing stroke, but his training held him back. Wariness and patience were weapons in the warrior's arsenal, as useful as sharpened steel. So it proved now. It was not a stumble, but a feint, and the assassin's blade twisted up in a disemboweling stroke even as his feet righted themselves. But his blade cut only the air.

Now was Gil's chance. His sword knocked aside his enemy's, and then drove forward taking the man in the neck. Blood spurted as one of the great arteries was severed, but the blade struck his spine too.

The man reeled back and convulsed. His eyes bulged; one hand clamped over his neck to stop the blood, but it sprayed through his fingers. A moment he stood thus, and then the life went out of him and he dropped to the floor. There he writhed for a few moments. His hand fell away from the wound, but the blood no longer spurted. His heart had ceased to beat.

Gil felt sick. He had killed him. He began to retch, but when he turned away from the sight the urge to vomit was less. A moment he stood there, the sweat all over his skin as cold as ice and the heaving breaths of air that he drew in like fire, but he forced himself to think and become calm.

What should he do now? Was the assassin's accomplice still on the other side of the door? Gil could almost feel his presence there. But that might just be fear giving life to his thoughts. He could cast forth his magic as he had intended before, but if the man was there it would not change anything.

It was time to act, and Gil did so. He swiftly grabbed a chair. It would serve as a shield from any arrow fired against him.

He took a deep breath and moved toward the door. It was better to take the initiative and confront whatever fate awaited him than stand still in fear and uncertainty.

8. You Shall be Rewarded

Ginsar bit her lip. A drop of blood slowly beaded there, and she tasted it upon her tongue. She looked at her hands, her long-fingered and beautiful hands. They were pale and trembling. Cold fear roiled in the pit of her stomach, and uncertainty gnawed at her. Was her premonition founded?

Soon, she would find out.

The acolyte walked toward her. His tread was slow and his head bowed. It was not a good sign. The coven made way for him, slipping aside like shadows to allow his passage.

But there was envy in their glances as they gave way, for he had been chosen above them all. Yet if he returned with ill-tidings or had failed in his mission, then he would suffer. This they knew also, for past experience had taught them that, and therefore yearning was in their gaze too. One less at the top of the order meant opportunity for them, as it had in times past.

Slow was the advance of the acolyte, and she smelled his fear. For once, it did not please her. She wanted news, and his tardiness was an irritant. Yes, one way or the other, he would suffer.

He came before her, and kneeled.

"Speak!" Ginsar commanded.

"Lady, I entered the city in disguise as you wished. I passed through the gate, and—"

"Fool!" Ginsar spat at him. "I do not need your prattling. Answer me this. Does Brand live?"

The man began to tremble. "Yes, Lady. I spoke with some who saw him return into the city with the boy."

So it was true.

Ginsar felt fury rise within her. How could this be? He was dead. She knew it. And yet in the hours that passed since she had seen his lifeless body her instincts warned her that somehow he lived. It was intolerable.

Carnhaina. Carnhaina! It was *her* doing. And there would be a purpose to it. And yet, was there not a way to gain from this? If Carnhaina had found a means of bringing back the dead, might Ginsar herself not do so? Could she return her Master and her brother into the world?

"What else?" she said, her voice cold and giving no sign of her thoughts.

"They say he is ill. Rumor is that his mind is broken."

"Rumor? I sent you to discover the truth, not rumor."

"Yes, Lady. But no one is sure of this."

"You are a fool. And the city is full of fools. Carnhaina has done this. Brand is not ill, nor is his mind broken. Not *him*."

She thought a moment. "What other rumors have you heard? Speak, and be heard!" She allowed anger to infuse her voice.

The acolyte groveled at her feet. The coven stepped back a pace, but their gazes intensified.

"The nobles rebelled, Lady. They tried to depose Brand, but their attempt failed. He is ... he is feared greatly. However, the boy now seems to rule. That is the word out of the palace. I have also learned—"

"Enough! It is all a ruse. Brand lives. Brand rules. Brand *still* schemes against me. Our enemy is not yet destroyed!"

Her fury ran free now, filling her voice and flashing from her eyes. And it burned her soul. *Shall such as Brand defy me?*

The acolytes backed further away, but they did not take their eyes off her. At her feet, the man trembled. He bobbed his head back and forth to the dirt, and inch by inch he began to withdraw. She stayed him with a touch of her boot, and he stilled as though the slightest movement could kill him. And it could.

Ginsar took pity on him. It was not his fault that he had brought unfortunate news. He had served her as best as he was able. Therefore, she would reward him. Yes, as indeed she would reward all her servants in the end. She would give every one of them what they deserved.

Her white teeth flashed in a sudden grin, and a throaty laugh followed. This disconcerted the coven even more. Mad, they thought her, but she would show them. And mad or not, they followed her for she gave them power. This was the lure that never failed, nor would it fail now. She would show them *power.*

She bent forward, and her long fingers ran through the hair of the man who prostrated himself before her. She breathed in of the air, dank and fetid as it was. She smelled the rank water that festered in the bottom of the grotto in which they had gathered.

The rocky sides of the steep-sided gully climbed about them. Ferns smothered it, hiding the treacherous paths down to this point. Above the sloping banks, tall pines grew and cast their shadows down as though from a great height. Everywhere was mold and slime and fungus.

Everything was damp. Ever the slow drip of water sounded, falling off leaf and stem and stone.

She breathed in of the air, and loved it. This was her natural haunt, a wild thing of magic at home where others dreaded to walk. And it was dark, dark as night even though the noonday sun shone on the world above. Oh yes. She shivered as she sensed it all. A dark place for dark magic, and she had the darkest at her command.

Tonight, she would invoke it.

Her hands ceased moving through the man's hair. "You shall be rewarded," she promised sweetly.

Slowly, the acolyte looked up.

Ginsar knelt and favored him with a kiss to the forehead. "You shall be rewarded, and will never need fear delivering bad news again."

She laid her hands firmly upon his head. A moment he looked at her, confused by what she had said, and then her hands stiffened.

The acolyte convulsed. His limbs thrashed and trembled. His fingers clawed the earth, ripping at dirt and stone. Foam appeared at his mouth and sprayed down to his chest. His eyes, filled with a wild fear, rolled in their sockets so that only the whites showed. But as swiftly as it all began, it ceased.

Ginsar withdrew her hands, and the man slumped to the ground and was still.

But he was not dead. One finger twitched ever so slightly. His eyes flickered behind the now-closed lids, and his chest rose and fell with breath.

With a fierce light in her gaze and a triumphant smile upon her face, Ginsar stood and looked around at the coven.

"He shall sleep until tonight," she told them. "And then you shall see the power that I have. You shall see, and the people of Cardoroth shall tremble in their sleep!"

9. A Glint in their Eye

Gil crept toward the door. He did not want to alert the assassin's accomplice that he was coming, but he could lose no time either. The accomplice would have heard the sword-fighting stop, but he would not know for certain who had won. Momentarily, there would be doubt. But the longer things went on the warier he would grow, because if the assassin had won he would swiftly make his escape.

With a chair in one hand, and the sword in his other, it would be hard to open the door. But he found that he could still use his sword hand to get a grip on the doorknob. There he paused, listening. All he heard though was the rush of blood in his own ears. There was nothing else.

He steadied himself for what was to come. This much at least he knew: he would not wait and cower. It was better to face his enemy, and if need be, sell his life dearly if it came to that.

He held high the chair and flung the door open. Swiftly, he dashed into the corridor, weaving as he moved rather than following a straight line and presenting an easy target.

His head snapped left and then right, but there was no one in the corridor. The accomplice had fled, no doubt hearing the fight within the room and fearing discovery.

Slowly, Gil put down the chair. He realized that his heart thudded in his chest and he felt dizzy. With a groan, he leaned back against the corridor wall. His heart slowed a little, but the dizziness did not improve. Then his body began to tremble.

Making sure once more that the corridor was truly empty, he slid his back down the wall until he was sitting. The trembling grew worse, and he gripped hard the hilt of the sword.

He knew he was lucky. Lucky to survive the first fight and lucky not to have to fight again. He breathed a long sigh of relief, but at just that moment he heard the rush of feet. There were several people at least. He staggered upright, still using the wall to support himself, and lifted his sword. If he were to die, he would die as a man.

Even as he fought to stay upright on trembling legs, the newcomers turned around the corridor to his left. They saw him straightaway, and they stopped. It was several Durlin, and Shorty and Taingern were at their head.

One look they gave him, assessing the situation in a glance. These were hard men. They saw the blood on his sword and knew he had survived an assassination attempt, survived it by himself. This was an achievement that took both courage and skill, and he saw recognition of that in their eyes. He was no longer a boy to them, and his pride soared.

The moment passed. In the next few seconds they were all around him and moving into the room to ensure no attackers were nearby.

"How did you know?" he asked Shorty.

The Durlindrath studied him a moment, making sure he was not wounded, then he answered.

"You have Elrika to thank for that. She ran into us, and hearing that you were safe and had returned from the forest she wanted to see you. We told her where you were. But when she got here she saw a strange man at guard at the door, and she began to worry. She came and got us. And we knew there was something badly wrong."

At that moment there was the sound of more rushing steps. It was Elrika herself, and she had fetched a knife that she held before her. She saw them all and paused. Her face was grim and her eyes flashed, and then she saw Gil. She looked at him, and then ran over.

They hugged fiercely, and Gil saw out of the corner of his eye Shorty and Taingern exchange a glance. Shorty winked at his friend, and Taingern raised an eyebrow. Gil ignored it all.

One of the Durlin came out of the regent's bedroom. "There's an assassin in there. A warrior by the looks of him. He's dead. And so is Rhodeurl, slain by an arrow."

Once more he felt the eyes of the Durlin on him. He had survived when their highly-trained comrade had not, and they knew that he either had great luck or had fought with skill and courage.

A Durlin came out of the room next to the regent's. "Parviel was killed and his body hidden in there, an arrow in his back."

The words were simple enough, but Gil knew that the two Durlin had died for him. They had survived Ginsar and the collapse of the cave only for this. He felt grief wash over him, and with it came guilt.

"Retrieve the bodies," Taingern said softly, "and bring them to the chapterhouse. We'll commence the funerary rites. They were good men, and we'll honor them as best we can."

"What of the other man?" Gil asked. "We can't let the accomplice get away."

"He's gone, Gil. But one way or another we'll find him. That much I promise. He must have fled as soon as he saw Elrika, guessing that she was fetching help."

10. Then You Must Go

Shorty and Taingern looked at him speculatively, and Gil was not quite sure why. Elrika was no longer hugging him, but she was standing very close.

Taingern was the one who broached the subject. "This is the first time you've ever killed anybody. It can be a difficult thing to come to grips with. Let us know if you would like to talk things over."

Gil thought about the assassin lying dead in the room just beside them, and he shuddered. It could just as easily be him in there.

"That man came to kill me, and he *would* have if I didn't kill him instead. He got what he deserved, and his death was his own fault."

"Perfectly true," Taingern agreed. "You had no choice, and what you did was right. Even so, that does not always help. Especially the first time. You may still experience feelings of guilt. You may wonder if you could have disarmed him instead. Your mind will throw it back at you again and again, and in different ways. There's a logical side to this … and an emotional one. They don't always match."

Gil felt Elrika's hand in his own, and he sensed she was worried for him. "So what's the solution to that?" he asked.

"Ah, Gil. There *is* no solution. But what helps you deal with it is this. Accept both sides of things. Yes, you did what you had to do. And yes, it will throw up emotional turmoil in your mind. Accept that both are valid, and in time you will move on."

It was an interesting perspective, and Gil liked it. "You know, you sounded a lot like Brand just then."

Taingern looked away, his thoughts seemingly elsewhere, but he answered promptly.

"Who was it, do you think, that years ago gave me the same advice?"

Gil paid close attention to Taingern's advice. The Durlindrath had been through life-and-death struggles worse than this several times. He had struggled to live against someone who sought his death, and no one knew what that was like unless they had been there. And Taingern was right. It was fitting to fight for your life, there was nothing wrong with it, but surviving still came at a cost.

Elrika slid the knife she carried through her belt. "I wish I'd had a sword. I could have helped you."

Shorty glanced hard at her for a moment, but he seemed to be remembering something rather than looking at her.

"I think the two of you should stay close for a while," he said. "And I think, Elrika, that you should carry a sword. You're a skilled fighter, and it never hurts to be prepared."

Gil liked the sound of that, and he knew he could trust her as well. And she really was skilled with a blade.

"Here," he said. "Take this one. It has a good feel and balance. I think you'll like it."

With a sure grip Elrika took the blade, looking at it curiously. "It does feel good, but it's an expensive weapon, better than anything I've used before."

The two Durlindraths exchanged a look.

"It's a fine blade indeed," Shorty said. "A princely gift, and it has a history that I'm guessing neither of you know."

Gil shook his head. "I just grabbed it from the wall when I needed it."

"It was given," Shorty said, "by the first king of Cardoroth to one of his sons. See the three stars engraved at the top of the blade? That signifies it was given to the third son. There were seven sons, and seven blades were given."

The history of the first king was coming back to Gil now. He had heard of those seven sons before.

"There were seven sons," he said. "Seven princes. But they were more than that. They were the first Durlin. They protected their father, and when he was attacked three died defending him."

"Exactly so," Taingern said. "But there is more."

There *was* more, and Gil remembered it. He softly intoned the Durlin creed:

Tum del conar – El dar tum!
Death or infamy – I choose death!

He turned to Elrika, but she spoke first. "I too know the history of the Durlin. It was the third son who spoke those words. He was one of the three who died."

She gazed at the sword in her hand, holding it now with reverence. Then she offered the hilt to Gil. "I have to give it back. This is too good a sword … there's too much history that comes with it. I'm just a baker's daughter."

Shorty and Taingern exchanged another look, and they seemed to reach an agreement.

"Take the sword, Elrika," Taingern encouraged. "It was a well-given gift, and you've earned it. I do not think that he who once bore it would be displeased. Nor would Brand. He thinks you would make a good Durlin. And we agree."

Gil sensed that something else was going on here. Somewhere deep in his mind he also had a feeling that this was meant to happen.

Elrika took the sword. "Tum del conar – El dar tum," she whispered.

"Thank you," Gil said to Shorty and Taingern. He looked around at the other Durlin. "Thank you all."

The Durlin bowed formally to him, a gesture he had not seen before from them.

"Walk with me, please," he said to Elrika.

They moved away, and several of the Durlin followed, silent and inscrutable as always. Gil did not travel far, though. They came to his room, and once there the Durlin entered first and searched it thoroughly before allowing the two of them to go inside.

His room was not as grand as the regent's, but it was nice enough and he saw Elrika study it. He offered her a chair near the window, and took one himself.

"I have learned something," he said. "At least I think I have."

He proceeded to tell her what he had found in Carnhaina's diary. He spoke of the section where she mentioned the four Riders, the gateways and the powers that form and substance the world. He repeated what she had written about those powers seeking balance, that if evil is born, so too is good and that it shall rise amid the shadows. He spoke of how she had said to look for it, for it was the key.

"But she said in none of this *where* to look," Elrika guessed.

"No, not at all. But then there was a drawing, a drawing of the Tower of Halathgar and the trapdoor at its bottom. I felt strongly then that that was where I had to go. But now, the feeling has passed. I'm not sure anymore."

"Well," she answered, "you must go anyway. Trust to your original instinct."

"But it was just a drawing … just a feeling."

"Trust your feelings, Gil. They're usually good."

He looked at her, suddenly glad that in all the world he had found her for a friend. And maybe his instincts were good, as she said. At any rate, he had nothing else to act on. This was a start, but it nagged at him that he could be wasting precious time.

11. Before Cardoroth

Night had fallen. Stars gleamed in the shadow-draped sky. Among them, bright Halathgar. The two-star constellation shimmed in the void, like eyes through a silken veil.

Closer to earth, a breeze blew. It bent the tops of the tall pines. In the boughs of those same trees crows roosted, and they cawed and croaked restlessly.

Gil had seen it all before. He had been here previously, and now as then he felt odd, for this was an odd place. Even the pale marks on his hand itched, as though the light from Halathgar woke something within him.

And, just as before, the Tower of Halathgar rose into the night. It seemed mysterious, all curves and crenellations, lit by starlight yet still shadowed by the night. It was a place of secrets, a place where secrets were revealed, and a place of death, for the great queen herself rested in her sarcophagus upon the pinnacle.

The Tower of Halathgar was also a lodestone for rumor. Stories were legion. It was a focal point of legend, even a relic of the ancient past amid the modern city, surrounded by living, breathing people and the hustle of a large population, and yet it remained remote as though its thousand-year history formed an unbroachable barrier all about it.

"It's as ugly as a pig with the pox," Shorty stated.

Taingern did not answer. He looked at the tower, stony-faced and grim. Gil did not say anything either, but he recognized Shorty's reaction. It was the time-honored warrior's way of reliving tension – make a joke. He wondered what Elrika would have thought, but she was not allowed to come. She was not yet a Durlin.

They approached the tower. Two guards stood there, uniformed in the livery of soldiers of Cardoroth. They watched closely, hands near the hilt of their swords, as the group drew close to them, and then there was recognition in their eyes. They bowed to Gil and saluted Shorty and Taingern.

"We need to go inside," Taingern said.

"Of course," one of the guards answered.

Quickly, the door was unlocked and opened. The group passed through. One of the soldiers gave Shorty a burning torch.

"Good luck in there," he said.

"Thanks. We may need it."

The door was closed behind them. They stood still a while, waiting for their eyes to adjust. Gil felt his heart thud, just as it had last time he came here. Shorty and Taingern gave no sign of nerves, but Gil knew they felt them all the same. They would normally have spoken with the soldiers and made them feel appreciated, but outside conversation had been minimal. They had other things on their mind.

Gil looked around. Ahead, the spiral staircase commenced the long wind to the top of the tower. He knew what lay there upon the pinnacle beneath the starlit sky. The trapdoor was another matter though. What was below it? How long had it been since anyone had ventured through?

"There it is," Gil said.

The others did not answer. Nor did they make a move toward it. It was visible now, a single plank of ancient wood, dust covered but set neatly within the floor. A long-rusted iron ring stood out from its center.

"Let's get this over with," Shorty said after a moment.

Taingern grinned at him. "One more adventure," he answered. "And think of it. Even Brand has not gone where we go now. He would be jealous!"

"There's truth in that." Shorty lifted the torch higher so it threw better light at the trapdoor. Taingern bent and took a grip of the iron ring. With a heave, he lifted the plank.

Dust filled the air as the trapdoor came free. Taingern lifted it clear easily, for though it was made of hardwood it was thin and relatively light. He placed it down again beside the opening that was now revealed.

Shorty stepped closer. The light from the torch flickered and wavered. It did little to illuminate things, but they could see enough. A vertical shaft lay before them, disappearing into blackness. There were wooden stairs too. These were more like wide ladder treads than stairs, but they spiraled down, disappearing into the blackness.

"I'll go first and test out the timber," Shorty offered, handing the torch to Taingern. "I'm light and nimble."

It was true, Gil knew, but he was lighter still. Shorty was trying to protect him, which was strange because there were no assassins here. Then again, none of them knew what other dangers there might be.

With sure but careful movements Shorty lowered himself into the shaft. Then he rested his weight on each tread gradually, testing them out one by one.

"So far so good," he said. "They feel quite solid."

Down he went, until his head was now below the level of the trapdoor and he could see the staircase properly.

"It's all good. Very solid and soundly made. I think you can start to follow me down."

Taingern gestured with his hand. "You first, Gil."

It was yet another indication that his two protectors were nervous about what was down here. There would be one ahead of him and one behind in case of trouble. But Gil did not argue.

He moved down, quicker than Shorty had started for now they knew the stairway was sound. But he still moved carefully.

Below he could see Shorty, but the light was not strong. Still, the Durlindrath seemed to be moving quite quickly now, confident that the timber would not give way.

Light flickered and dust floated through the air as Taingern also entered the shaft. The smell of smoke from the torch grew stronger, but Gil was glad of it. This was not a place he wanted to be in the dark.

The shaft did not continue long. Soon, the ladder-like stairway brought them to a flat section of ground. They could not see much, but the shaft widened somewhat and plunged ahead, horizontally this time, into the dark.

They moved forward. The ground before them was covered deep by dust, but there were tracks there of at least one person.

"Did you explore ahead?" Taingern asked.

"No," Shorty answered. "They're not mine."

Gil was surprised, even alarmed. "Who else could have come here? Do you think they might be somewhere ahead?"

Shorty shook his head. "I don't think so. It's hard to tell, but those tracks could be weeks old. Maybe even years or centuries. Who can say? I get the feeling that nothing much changes down here, and there's no breeze to blow dust to cover any marks. For all I know, they might be the tracks of Carnhaina herself."

That was something that Gil had not realized. This place was ancient, and there was nothing to mark the passage of years or obliterate tracks. Perhaps, in a hundred years or so, someone would one day look at their own tracks and wonder who had made them and why.

They moved forward. It was hard to tell distances in the dim light, and their slow passage did not help. Gil felt a sense of timelessness as well, which was disorientating, but they had moved well away from the tower.

After perhaps a hundred feet they came to a door. It was made of wood, but either it was constructed of a different kind than the trapdoor or there was more moisture in the air here, because it was falling apart. Some of the boards that made it up had holes in them, and it sat at an angle on one hinge, part way open.

Very carefully, Shorty moved it. Several chunks of rotted timber fell away like moldy dust, but it stayed on the one hinge that supported it. Now, there was a big enough gap to pass through. Shorty did not hesitate.

The corridor widened from this point. Rugs covered the floor, or at least what was left of them. They were nearly rotted away. The walls were also covered. Tapestries hung there, and these were in better condition than the rugs. Some had fallen, and some were mold and lichen crusted, but many were still in fair condition.

The air was stale and unpleasant. It stank of rot. None of this stopped Shorty though. He moved forward, his head turning from side to side as he went, looking at the relics of the past or, more likely, checking for dangers.

Gil and Taingern followed. They did not speak, for this was not the kind of place for conversation. It was best to follow Shorty's example and move ahead slowly and cautiously.

They were further away from the tower now, perhaps somewhere under city buildings or beneath the tree-filled park near the tower.

Shorty slowed. "It's another door," he whispered.

This one was better preserved, though Gil could not understand why. It seemed to be made just as the previous one had been. The only difference was that this one had strange symbols carved into it.

"Do you recognize any of those marks?" Taingern asked.

"No, I've never seen them before."

"Does it look like it could be lòhrengai of some sort?"

"No, I don't think so. I've never heard of lòhrens using writing in their magic. At least, Brand never taught me anything like it. Some will speak in the Halathrin language when they invoke power ... but this is not Halathrin script."

"No matter," Taingern said. "I just have a feeling that there is magic of some sort here, or at least there once was."

Gil had the same feeling. It might explain why the door was better preserved. Some power might still linger here. He could seek it out and find it with his own, but that might wake it from dormancy and it was best to leave things just as they were.

Shorty opened the door. The hinges still worked, but dust filled the air. As they moved through, Gil saw that within the carved symbols was the remnant of color. Once, they had been painted. Were they meant to stand out, perhaps as a warning of some kind?

They went into the chamber beyond. This was a square, and ancient benches lined the walls. People had gathered here for some purpose, or waited. The benches were once solid, but rot had set into them. Gil ran his finger along one, and chunks of timber disintegrated at his touch. Why had the door not rotted in the same way?

Ahead, another staircase began. They went to it and commenced to descend once more. Deeper into the earth they went, and it was hard to know just how far underground they now were. There was no noise save for what they made themselves, and this they tried not to do.

It was silent. The air itself seemed oppressive, though it was neither hot nor cold. There was no life here, not even insects seemed to survive in the century-old darkness. And then, without any warning, the surroundings changed.

Shorty paused. He looked around. "This is no longer a part of the tower," he said softly. "We're now in a natural tunnel."

"I think much of what we've passed through since coming down the trapdoor was built *before* the tower," Taingern suggested. He brushed off a layer of fine dust that had settled on his hand from the torch. "But this is older still."

It was an interesting thought, but one that Gil found disturbing. It raised a question for which he had no answer. The tower was old, dating back near to the foundation of the city. How then could there be man-made tunnels beneath it that were older? And if they were, who built them?

His mind moved back to the symbols on the door. He had never seen them before, nor their like. Perhaps that was because they had not been inscribed by his people at all, but by someone who lived here before the Camar settled these lands. If so, who were they? And why did they build these tunnels in the rock?

There were no answers, and they moved ahead. But they did not go far before Gil glimpsed something that disturbed him again.

"Look," he said, and pointed to the wall on their left.

Taingern moved the torch closer, and what Gil had glimpsed was revealed in full. There were more symbols there, this time carved into the stone.

"It's not like anything that I've seen before," Shorty said.

"Nor me," Taingern agreed.

Gil studied them closely. "I don't think it's the same as what was on the door. It looks different."

Taingern peered at the marks. "I think you're right. This is something else again."

"It's almost…" Gil hesitated, not quite sure if he were right. "It's almost like writing."

The torch gutted, and then it flared brighter. He saw more clearly now. "I'm sure of it. It's writing."

"It's not Camar though," Taingern said. "It's nothing like it."

"No," Gil answered. "But it's writing, and I think I now know who did it."

They turned to him, and in the flickering light he saw the curiosity in their eyes.

"Once," he said, "there was a race of people who held dominion over the land. It was long ago. None of the books I've ever read could say exactly when their empire began or when it ended, but it was long before the Camar came east. Long, long before that. Have you heard of them?"

Shorty nodded slowly. "I have. There are a few tales told about them by bards. It's hard to know what's true and what isn't."

"I too have heard of them," Taingern said. "Brand knows more than us, and he has spoken of them occasionally."

Gil was glad that they knew. His theory made sense, and it seemed possible, even likely, that Cardoroth was founded on the same place that some of the Letharn had chosen to live, that ancient race that once ruled much of Alithoras. But it did not answer the question of what this place was, and what they used it for.

"Best to keep going," Shorty said. "Letharn or not, these corridors lead somewhere, and it can't be much further."

They walked forward, and Shorty was proven correct within another twenty or so paces.

The torchlight fluttered once again. It went dark, and then as the light sprang up brighter a kind of portal was revealed, and a stele before it.

The portal was triangular in shape. Beyond was darkness. Before the portal the stele stood, squat and ugly. This was what drew Gil's attention. It was as tall as a man, but wider than it was high. Each of its four faces was inscribed with the same writing they had seen earlier.

He went over to look, and the others followed. The marks on the stone were easy to see here. They were a series of dots, slashes and half circles, obviously writing but different from anything he had ever seen before.

Gil was fascinated. The stele had an ancient and brooding presence. And though the script was clear, the stone was very, very old. It even showed signs of weathering, by rain or wind. Neither was possible in its present location. He walked around it to see what was on the other faces. All of them were inscribed, but on the one nearest the portal there were two sets of inscriptions: the top in the same script as the rest, and the bottom, much to Gil's surprise, in ancient Camar.

He could read it. He had learned this older version of Cardoroth's present language. He supposed that Shorty and Taingern could work their way through it as well, but not as fluently as he could. He read it out for them, his voice soft, but the hollow chamber took his words and hissed them back at him.

Attend! We are masters of the world. We possess the wealth of nations. Gold adorns our hands; priceless jewels our brows; bright are our swords. The world shudders when we march! But heed well that other powers are older and greater than we. Herein is one. He that is with power may invoke it. If he dares.

12. Filled with Terror

Night fell over the grotto and Ginsar grew excited. Moths flittered through the air, and the bats that hunted them wheeled and spun after their prey. But for all that death, for all that movement, it was silent. It seemed unnatural, and then even the moths and bats disappeared, taking their deadly game elsewhere. The grotto was still. At a signal from her, the acolytes stood and filed toward where she stood from their place of rest.

She waited. No words were spoken. None were needed. They had all seen this before.

She began to chant. It was soft at first, drawing forth the power that rested dormant within her, but also seeking out and joining to it the power that slumbered in the surrounding earth and air. Her voice became one with the night. It was a dark thing, full of the unexpected, imbued with the watchfulness of prey and the stealth of the hunter.

At her feet, the chosen acolyte stirred. He could not move nor speak, but his eyes rolled in their sockets. He too knew what was to come. There was horror in his eyes and the twist of his mouth, and tears streamed down his face. He saw his death in her gaze, and that he was powerless to prevent it fueled his terror.

Ginsar looked upon him, and his dread uplifted her. She fed upon it, making it one with her chanting and the dark night. Her heart swelled, and the power within her waxed greater.

Her chanting grew louder, filling the grotto and reverberating through the stone banks that bulked all about them in the dark. It snaked up the trunks of the tall pines, and their long leaves shivered in the starlight like a million daggers.

The acolytes drew closer, eager to see what was to come. Glee was on their faces and malice in their hearts. It could have been them, but it was *him* instead, and they liked that.

A cloud drifted across the sky, blocking out the stars and plunging the grotto into darkness so profound that it seemed impossible light could ever have existed. She snapped her fingers and one of the acolytes lit a torch that spluttered to life with ruddy light. The dark was good, but better still to see the transformation she would now work, and the sorcery that gave it life.

Ginsar's chanting rose to a crescendo, and then it ceased with the abruptness of a knife cut. In the sudden silence she reached out and placed a hand upon her chosen sacrifice. Then her hand slowly lifted, and the acolyte rose up before her as though pulled by an invisible rope.

Slowly, as though she had all eternity for the action, she reached to her side and drew a knife from her robe. It was a wicked looking blade, curved like a sickle moon and etched with runes that gleamed amid the dark with eldritch light. It felt good in her hand.

The acolyte's mouth worked soundlessly. Gently, she touched his head. In response, he tilted it back and exposed his throat. Almost lovingly, she caressed the flesh with the knife. A thin red line appeared. Then blood beaded and trickled down his pale skin.

The man's eyes bulged. There was pleading in them. She drank that in and cut deeper. Blood spurted now. Red, vivid, intoxicating to her as wine.

Ginsar shuddered. The knife slid a little deeper, and a crimson spray erupted from the pulsing artery. Slowly, she pushed the man down to the ground. He could not resist. There she had set a small basin of metal. It was dark and empty. Soon though, it filled with the acolyte's life-blood. Spasms jerked his body, and then he slumped fully to the ground. The blood ceased to spray as his heart stilled.

She ignored the dead body. What mattered now was the blood in the basin. She studied it, marveling at the sheen on its surface and the strange play of light that gleamed and glistened as the swirling fluid congealed.

13. A Past Age

Gil knew that it was time he took the lead. This was his quest, given him by Carnhaina herself, and he would follow it. Now, it led him toward the triangular portal, and he moved forward.

Shorty made to step in front of him, but Gil placed a hand on his shoulder.

"Not this time, my friend. The time has come for me to grow up."

Shorty hesitated. "So be it. But be careful. We don't know what's down there."

Beyond the portal Gil discovered a natural cave. There was nothing man-made about it at all. The floor dipped and rose, the walls were irregular and the flickering light of the torch cast many-angled shadows. From the domed roof grew stalactites, wet with moisture and gleaming yellow-white from the torch light. And here and there on the ground rose stalagmites like the arms of dead men spearing up from the earth.

The cave was eerie and disconcerting, but there was something else that disturbed Gil even more. The city was somewhere above them, no more than a hundred feet or so away, but this was another world and it was entirely remote and alien from anything he knew. And there was *power* here.

Now, he must cast forth his own and discover it. He must find its source, for that was why they had come. He signaled the others to stand still and then allowed the lòhrengai within him to stir, to reach out and seek what was in the cave.

His senses became far more acute, and he heard the drip of water from somewhere nearby and his eyes pierced the gloom beyond the reach of the torch light.

Straightaway, he found the source of power that filled the cave, and his eyes locked upon it. He could see it, yet he did not think the others could. He moved forward again, cautiously, and the two Durlindraths stayed close at his side.

In the center of the domed cave lay a small basin, about the size of a long stride. It had been delved into the stone by the hand of man, or at least someone at some time had taken what nature provided and evened out its shape.

The stone of the basin was dark, and its rounded lip polished to a gleam all about its perimeter. Within, lay a sheet of water, impossibly still as though caught out of time. Nothing moved within it, nor caused its surface to break. Yet reflected from its mirror-like surface was all the ceiling of the cave, the glint of long-pointed stalactites and the shadow-pocked surface of the cave roof. But from deep within, light stirred and ebbed, reacting to the flicker of torch light.

"It's a scry basin," whispered Gil to the others. They studied it, but did not answer.

Brand had once told him of them, and Gil had read of them also. They were a thing of ill-name, for sorcerers used them. Ginsar, he recalled, had one. But this was not of that kind. There was no sacrifice here, no blood nor residue of evil.

Gil looked up. Directly above the basin was a stalactite. It gleamed with moisture, and at its dagger-like tip a single drop of water hung suspended. It was this that fed the

75

basin, though it was impossible to say how often that drop fell. It might be poised there for hours or even days before it fell.

Gil sensed the age of the thing. Old, old as time. The basin had lain here since before the Camar, since before the Letharn. It had begun to fill when the world was young, and the power of magic that coursed through the earth was strong within it: ùhrengai, the primordial force whence the sorcery of elùgai and the enchantment of lòhrengai both sprung.

But that was not the only power that hung in the air. All about him Gil now sensed the remnants from once-mighty spells of a past age. The feel of the magic was not quite like his own, but he recognized it. It reminded him of Brand's staff, the one that the great lòhren Aranloth had given him.

Clearly, Carnhaina had discovered this place and she had used it. He felt the residue of her power also, somewhere between sorcery and enchantment. This was why her tower was built where it was, to allow access to the basin and to hide it.

And that sparked a question. Carnhaina had used it, but could he? Did he have the power? And if he did, what might he learn to give direction to his quest?

14. A Red Mist

The eyes of the dead acolyte glinted. Ginsar ignored them. With a flick of her knife she deepened the wound in his neck, and a last trickle of blood dribbled into the basin.

Ginsar breathed in of the night air. Life felt good, and power coursed through her. She suddenly laughed with the joy of it, and then sobered quickly. There was more work yet to do.

Gently, reverently, she removed the basin and allowed the corpse to settle to the ground. She sensed the eyes of the acolytes upon her, watching wide-eyed with anticipation. They knew what came next, for they had seen it before.

Ignoring the coven, she studied the basin. The life-blood within it had already begun to thicken. Carefully, she stirred it with the blade of her knife. But her deft movements were not random. She shaped runes with each cut and stroke of the blade. Letters formed, and then dissolved back into the blood. But the power she drew forth remained, and slowly grew.

In the grotto, the air began to turn cool. An icy breeze stirred, sucking heat from those gathered there, and they pulled their cloaks tightly about them. Above, the dim tops of the pine trees were still.

Ginsar began to mutter as her blade moved through the blood. Her words were harsh and guttural, and as she spoke them she heard in her mind her master utter them also. Shurilgar had taught her what to say, and his voice resonated now with her own.

She chanted louder now, no longer muttering but fiercely casting the words into the air. The blade in her hand grew hot to touch, and a sudden wind roared to life and flew through the grotto. Now, the tops of the pines began to lurch and sway. The wind howled among the trunks, and in the grotto the hollows between stones screeched and groaned.

And then there was more. There was a voice, and Ginsar felt the touch of something otherworldly on her mind.

"Come!" she commanded. "Come hither. You are called!"

Steam, red-tinged and ethereal, rose from the basin of blood. The wind took it and dashed it madly into the air. The voice answered, cold and remote.

"I come, Ginsar. I come, and your world shall tremble."

The blood in the basin thickened. The knife now stirred it with great difficulty. Steam continued to rise from it, but the wind no longer dashed it away. It formed around Ginsar like a cloak.

The wind died. The trees stilled. The moaning from the rocks ceased, and the steam churned. Mist-like, it swirled through the air, flowing around Ginsar, twining about her limbs and caressing her face.

She trembled at its touch, feeling the power that she summoned, breathing it in and exhaling it, becoming one with it.

The acolytes fell to the ground, awed by what she had done, fearful of the dread power that had come among them. Even Ginsar felt a twinge of panic, for she sensed the hunger of the spirit she had summoned. Her body would serve as host better than the one she had prepared for that purpose, and the spirit-thing sensed it too. It probed her, tested the strength of her sorcery and the vigor of her mind.

Her heart thrashed in her chest. Goosebumps formed on her skin, and the muscles of her body tensed like cords of iron. She flung the congealed blood from the basin down onto the dead acolyte.

Blood must follow blood, and the summoning must leave her and enter the corpse. She felt its resistance to the pull, and then with a last caress it left her and sped like an arrow into the dead acolyte.

The red mist clung to him. It knifed into his flesh, and his head jerked back. His body twitched and spasmed, then thrashed in wild convulsions.

Ginsar stepped back. The acolytes watched in horrified satisfaction. He who had once been their brother was changing.

The corpse screamed. Its skin tore where muscles bulged. Its eyes popped. Even bones cracked, jagged edges showing before knitting together again in an altered shape.

This was more than Ginsar had expected. The body before her was reshaping, changing and forming into something new. The previous Rider had not done this.

The body stilled. It lay hunched over on the ground. Then a hand reached out, and it levered itself upright. Slowly, it stood. The acolyte was gone, though the robes that once he had borne still clung, ragged and bloody, to the creature that now stood there.

Even Ginsar was horrified. This was more than she had sought, but it was *hers*. Hers to command and use as she pleased. Hers to send against her enemies.

A slow smile spread over her face. How her enemies would fear *this*. Ah, life was sweet. For all who opposed her must soon fall, and her power was growing. She felt it swirl within her now, coursing through her body like the red blood that thrummed in her heart.

15. Knives in his Back

Gil knelt beside the basin. Shorty and Taingern kept close. The water in the pool was still as glass, reflecting all that lay above, but showing nothing of what lay within. It was strange, for it must be only shallow, and he should be able to catch a glimpse of its bottom, but there was nothing. Perhaps it was deeper than it seemed.

He dismissed these thoughts from his mind. What mattered now was what he could do with it.

"Be careful," Taingern said.

Gil nodded, but did not answer. Careful of what? Certainly, there were dangers here. There were dangers wherever great power was concentrated. But he did not know enough about what this place was to know what the dangers were. He would have to find out, bit by bit, as he went. But that was a dangerous process in itself…

He cast his senses out, letting the lòhrengai within him expand, letting it go where it was drawn. But nothing happened. The tendrils of magic probed the basin, felt the age of the stone and the power within the water, and though they were drawn to it, they were rebuffed from the still surface as though it were made of stone.

This was something Gil had never encountered before. He thought a moment, unsure of his next step. Magic was a thing of the mind rather than the body, but that was not working here. Should he touch it?

Unsure, he reached out. Shorty and Taingern tensed beside him. With the deftest movement of a finger, he touched the surface of the water.

He felt nothing unusual. The water was cool to touch, and the reflections within it danced and shivered, but nothing else changed.

Tentatively, he allowed several fingers to break the surface. His lòhrengai reached out from them to plumb the water, but everything seemed muted and he could not detect any change or means by which the power of the pool might be summoned. Was it even a scry basin after all? It was possible that he was missing something obvious, but he could not think of anything.

Had he been wrong to touch the water? A scry basin showed images, and still water was necessary for that. But he had not been able to invoke its power when it was still, and its use as a conduit of visions came not just from the water but also from the power that resided in the soil, rock and air all through the cave.

He lowered his hand deeper into the basin. Strangely, he felt no bottom. Reaching down further, he slid in his arm until it was elbow deep.

He felt foolish, and he knew Shorty and Taingern were watching him, wondering what he was doing and if he had sufficient skill to invoke the magic that was bound to this place. He tried yet again to send tendrils of lòhrengai from his fingers, but his probing remained muted.

The water was different to his touch though. Once he was below the surface layer, it turned blood warm. It felt pleasant, and the mark on his palm tingled. Yet still, nothing happened. It was as though he were trying to run over ice. He could gain no traction, and nothing was working. Everything he was doing was wrong, but why?

His lòhrengai should be able to join with the existing lòhrengai that the ancient Letharn had created. He should be able to join with it, and then activate it. Why could he not do that simple thing?

The answer came to him, and he withdrew his arm from the water and looked up at his companions.

"I've been a fool. I knew I was missing something obvious."

"We all do, lad, from time to time. Have you worked out now how it works?"

"I have. I was trying to use lòhrengai to invoke the power here. But this isn't lòhrengai. It's ùhrengai, the primordial power from which both lòhrengai and elùgai derive. This scry basin was made before those terms meant anything. The power here is primitive. It's not invoked and turned toward a purpose … it's unleashed, for want of a better word. Watch now, but be careful for I have no real control over what will happen."

Gil dipped his hand into the water once more. He did not bother to send out his lòhrengai into it, rather he felt the ùhrengai and allowed it to enter him.

He swirled his hand in the water, and he felt the primordial powers that formed and substanced the world gather into the vortex of the water. His senses ventured into it, not trying to control or bring order, but just to become one with it.

His palm tingled and the water grew heavy. He did not swirl it fast nor slow, but gradually increased the speed until the vortex increased. He was one with it, swirling with it, and then, slowly, the greater power that infused the whole cave began to ebb and flow, twisting through the air as though one with the water. And Gil was in the center of both forces, the conduit for powers ancient as the rocks of the earth itself.

He felt giddy, as though his mind also spun. But he did not fight it. He allowed it all into him, and he became the water, the air and the rock. He was here now in the present, but he felt that he was also falling, falling deep into the past as well. Everything was one, and he was one with everything.

The water in the basin seethed and steamed, and he withdrew his hand. Sparks dripped from his fingers. He ignored them, ignored the steam and watched the water carefully.

The steam subsided. It seemed now that the water was still and the cave swirled about him. He continued to watch, and in the water lights flickered and images formed.

Shorty and Taingern did not move, but the breath hissed from their mouths. A grotto appeared in the water, dark and gloom-filled. Tall pines shadowed it. The rock was slick with moisture and ferns grew from cracks and crevices.

The vision was black as midnight, but a sickly glow spread from its center. Ginsar stood there, tall and terrible. He would know her anywhere. About her were gathered her acolytes. They had prostrated themselves before their mistress, but one of their number rose from where he had lain at her feet.

The figure stood. His every movement was lithe and graceful. He seemed young and lively, though there was a broody darkness to his eyes that spoke of long years of discontent. Golden hair spilled down around his shoulders. He turned a little, looking around him, and Gil gasped.

84

Sticking from the man's back were knives. They were lodged deep, seeming a part of him, for they moved when he moved. And blood dripped from each wound, trickling down the back of his cloak.

Gil remembered Carnhaina's warning. This was not a man, but another Rider.

"Betrayal," he whispered.

Taingern and Shorty drew their blades, as though ready to strike. He held up a hand to them.

"Watch. And do not touch the water!"

Gil studied the Rider. There was as yet no horse, but he knew that would come. As though from a great distance, he began to sense more about the thing that had been summoned.

It now inhabited the body of one of the acolytes, but there was more than that. Gil felt also a sense of opening, a passageway between worlds. He could not see it, but he intuited it was there. It loomed like a gaping hole in something that was once solid, and he wondered that Ginsar evidenced no sense that it existed. That it had been created, she must know, but that it had failed to close completely she seemed unaware.

Carnhaina was right. Other things sought to enter beside the Rider that had been summoned. He felt their shadowy presence, and fear rose within him.

The water of the scry basin shimmered. It seemed that the darkness of the grotto grew, and then suddenly there was a shiver of light and he looked upon a different scene.

A face came into focus. An old face. A woman's face. Her nut-brown face crinkled in what might have been an irritated expression. Her rheumy eyes glanced around as though seeking something unseen. About her shoulders was a threadbare shawl, and her short, coarse hair was

85

lank. The sun-beaten skin of her brow furrowed, and suddenly her glance focused on Gil. She was looking straight at him.

She grunted, though there was no sound, and a bony hand waved through the air. Even as she moved, the scry basin hissed and spat water. Gil caught a glimpse of another face, this one young and beautiful but strangely serene. Then the water returned to its glass-like state. The visions had ceased.

Shorty broke the silence. "The seer!" he hissed.

"Who was the man?" Taingern asked.

"The man," answered Gil, "was one of the Riders that Carnhaina foretold. Betrayal. She warned of his coming. But I don't know the others."

"The old lady was a seer," Shorty told him. "Brand has met her. She's famous, but very cantankerous. She lives outside the West Gate."

"And what of the young girl?" Gil said.

The others knew nothing of her, but it was her that intrigued Gil the most. How could such a young face appear so tranquil, so wise and at peace with the world? There was a mystery there, and he hoped to unravel it.

Shorty must have seen the curiosity on his face. "Time will tell, lad. It always does. One day you shall know who she is, but likely enough she will prove to be nothing like what you're expecting. It's always the way."

What Shorty said was true, and Gil knew it. "You're right. So, let's concentrate on what we *do* know. This much seems clear at any rate ... Ginsar has summoned the second Rider. At least, if the basin showed the present rather than the future. He will come against us. And that is likely to be soon. What else have we learned?"

"The seer has a true gift," Taingern answered. "It may be that she can help us. We should seek her out."

"Oh, she has power alright," Gil said. "She knew she was being watched, and she didn't like it. Not only did she discern the magic of the scry basin, but she dispelled it with great casualness. Not even Ginsar did that."

As soon as Gil spoke though, another thought occurred to him. If the seer knew she was being watched, perhaps Ginsar had as well. She might have allowed him to see what she wanted him to, or even manipulated it in some way. He was not sure if that was possible, and he had no time to think about it.

"And the young lady?" asked Taingern. "What can we deduce about her?"

Gil turned his mind to the question. "Very little," Gil replied. "But the basin does not show images at random. The scry magic is one with the user's mind, and it shows what the user needs to see. Whoever she is, she will prove important by the end. And I think, one way or the other, the seer will lead us to her."

16. All things have their Opposite

They returned to the palace through the quiet streets. It was dark and subdued, for there seemed no revelers. Perhaps it was too late, because the night was nearly done. The gray of dawn had begun to slip through the streets even as did they.

By the time they reached the palace grounds, bright sunlight shone and the sky was brilliant blue. Gil marveled that it could dawn so fine a day when he knew what darkness lay ahead. Betrayal was coming, the second Rider, and evil would follow in his wake.

They were in the grounds now, the gardens all about them. The paving was clean beneath their boots, the grass well clipped and the shrubbery to their left in full flower. Here and there guards patrolled, and he knew that others were stationed in various towers, watching keenly day and night for intruders. Even so, Shorty and Taingern did not let their guard down. They stayed close as they proceeded, their eyes casually assessing everything they saw for signs of danger.

They drew near to the palace. Gil was preoccupied. What would Ginsar do? In what way would the Rider attack them? He did not know any of these things, and that worried him. How could he defend against the unknown? It was troubling, and it also gave him a glimpse into the lives of his grandparents. During their reign, it had been much the same, year after year and decade after decade. The nobility were fools, for they sought to be kings themselves. How swiftly they would tire of the burden!

There was movement in the shadow beneath some trees. Gil had just seen it, but the two Durlindraths who could not have seen it any sooner reacted faster than he would have believed possible. Their blades hissed from their sheaths and they sprang before him.

"You won't need those, boys," a voice said dismissively. "Put them away."

Neither Shorty nor Taingern moved. From beneath the trees a figure emerged into the sunlight. She shuffled forward, seemingly aged and arthritic, leaning on a walking stick. But Gil was not fooled. There was strength in her body yet. He saw it in her eyes.

"Put them down, I say."

The two Durlindraths lowered their weapons, but they did not sheath them.

"I know you, lady," Shorty said. "You are the seer."

"Bah! You know me not at all. And it's better that way. But yes, you can call me that if you like. I don't really care."

"How did you get into these grounds?" Taingern asked.

The old woman fixed him with a rheumy stare, but there was iron in her gaze.

"Who could stop me?"

"There are guards and watchmen everywhere."

"Whoop-de-do!" she cackled. "I walk where I will. At least, wherever these old legs will carry me."

She nimbly hopped on one foot and mimicked using the walking stick to keep her balance. Then she bowed to the Durlindrath. When she straightened, she gazed straight at Gil and all sense of humor was gone from her face.

"Hail, king to be. And well met."

"Greetings, lady." Gil offered her his most eloquent bow.

"Ha! I see that Brand has taught you manners. Good for you." She stared at him closely, and he felt that her gaze saw right through him. "And he has taught you more besides. That is clear too."

He knew exactly what she meant. Magic. Though how she could tell, he was not sure. He sensed none about her, but he was willing to bet she possessed great talent.

"You are correct, lady."

She grinned at him impishly. "I'm no lady. If you knew my story ... well, never mind. Call me lady if it pleases you."

"Who are you then?"

"Just an old, old woman."

"And is that all?"

"Is it not enough?"

"Of course," Gil said.

She grinned at him. "I'm a seer also."

"That much, lady, I knew."

She stepped closer to him, and then pinned him once more with her stare.

"Would you like to know your future?"

"Perhaps."

She clapped her hands together, somewhat like a child who is greatly pleased.

"Ah. You are *so* like Brand. He was reluctant too."

"And you told him his?"

"I told him some, but not all. Oh, he is a great one, he is. Yes. And fate has only just begun with him. But now, now is your moment, king to be."

She studied him carefully, and he felt uncomfortable but tried not to show it. She laughed, as though she understood his every thought.

"Then what would you tell me, lady?"

"What would you like to know?" she countered.

Gil was uncertain. He had never met anyone like her.

90

The old woman cackled. "You are not ready, boy. But you have seen much, and there is power in you. Oh yes! My eyes see what others don't. Yes, there is power in you boy. This much I will say. Seek Brand. He will tell you."

"Brand is … ill."

"He is not. He's fine. He withdraws, that is all. His time in Cardoroth is coming to an end. Seek him and learn."

"Is that all you would tell me? What of Carnhaina?"

"Ah. Her quest."

Gil knew then, beyond doubt, that she was a true seer. Very few knew of the quest, and she had no ordinary means to discover anything about it.

"Yes," he said.

"You will be savior. Or you will be destroyer. You will be the Light, or you will be the Dark."

"I will always be of the Light," he said quickly.

She slowly shook her head. "Foolish boy! Stupid. You know so little of the world, but you are learning."

He ignored that. "How shall I close the gateway between worlds that Carnhaina warned of? How shall I fulfill my quest?"

"Oh, you still have so *much* to learn. You? You cannot do it."

Gil straightened. "I must. And I will."

The old woman leaned on her walking stick, and looked at him as though she were seeing him for the first time.

"You know, I see your grandfather in you. Yes, I see it. But you're wrong. You can't do it. You don't have the power. No one does."

"Then you think the world is lost?"

"Did I say that, boy? Listen. You don't have the power. None in Alithoras does. But think of this. Brand has taught you that all things have their opposite, has he not? All forces, once set in motion, have a result. And consequences breed consequences. He will have told you these things, or something like them, yes?"

"He has," Gil agreed.

"He will also have said this. The powers that form and substance the world seek balance. Always. Ceaselessly."

"Yes," he said.

"Then think, boy!"

"On what?"

She raised her walking stick and pointed it at him. "Typical! The young can be so wise and stupid at the same time. They have so much energy, so much time, and are so quick to ask questions instead of think for themselves. Worse, when they are given answers, they believe them. Foolish!"

"I need your help, lady."

"Ha! I'm too old to help. Too old to care. The world can look after itself without me."

"I need you."

"Figure it out yourself, boy. Prove yourself worthy of Carnhaina's trust. But know this. War comes. Armies march. Cardoroth must fight once again if it is to live. Already I hear the battle crows caw."

She tapped a finger to her head, and pulled her shawl higher over her shoulders. Then she hobbled off into the shadows of the trees again. Gil took a few steps after her, but like smoke on the wind she had disappeared.

It was then that he understood. She had never been here at all, not in person at least.

He turned back to Taingern and Shorty. "What would she have me do?"

They studied the shadows where she had disappeared carefully, and then sheathed their blades.

"I have no idea," Taingern answered.

"Nor me," Shorty said.

One thing Gil knew. The seer had not come to him for no purpose. For all her bluster, she had offered help. In her own way perhaps, but help still. Somewhere in her words was the answer he needed.

17. Cardoroth Needs You

"What now?" Shorty asked.

Gil was not sure. The seer had not told him anything that he did not already know, and yet that only meant that the answers to his questions were within his reach, if he could but see clearly.

He realized that was not quite true. She had said that Brand was well. He was not, not at all. And yet what she said was possible. Perhaps he was withdrawing…

"We will see Brand," he said.

"A good place to start," Taingern agreed. "Always, he seems to be at the heart of everything."

They entered the palace. While they walked through the corridors, Gil had more time to think. Just as on the journey back from the forest, the two Durlindraths were letting him lead. He realized now that they wanted to let him feel the pressure of responsibility. That way they would see what he was made of. And he would discover it for himself, too. One day he would lead the realm, and this was their way of getting him used to it, of training him for the job.

He could not blame them. He *should* be tested. If he proved unworthy, then someone else should lead, for trouble was coming. But he would prove to them that he *was* worthy.

The thought occurred to him that in proving to the others that he was ready, he would prove it to himself. This was also part of their plan. And certainly, if he could fulfill the charge that Carnhaina had given him, he would be worthy to lead Cardoroth. Was she also testing him? Was that how life worked? Every step forward, every choice, a test?

They came to the area of the palace set aside for healing. This was Arell's domain, where she offered help to the population of the city, especially those who could not afford it or those that other healers within the city could not help.

They passed through the passageways. On either side of the corridors were rooms with beds. Some were empty, but there were sick people here too. They moved quietly so as not to disturb them. Brand, no doubt, would be close to Arell's office.

They entered the last corridor. A nurse passed by them, busy on some errand, but she smiled at Shorty. Taingern raised an eyebrow.

"You know her?"

Shorty shrugged. "I think she stitched a wound for me, once."

He hurried on, and they quickly came to the last room. It was full of people, the sickest of the sickest, for that way they would be close to Arell, but Brand was not among them.

"Let's try Arell's office," Shorty suggested.

There was one more room at the end of the corridor, but this one had a door. It was closed.

Gil stepped forward and knocked on it.

"Enter," came Arell's voice.

They walked inside. Arell and Brand were seated at a table. Gone was Brand's dazed look, and he seemed acutely alert. He was dressed in fine clothes, but he wore a chainmail hauberk and his Halathrin blade was sheathed at his side. He looked fit and ready to go, ready for anything that life might throw at him. Yet there was a look in his eye that Gil could not interpret. The man had died and been brought back to life. It had changed him in some way, but Gil had no frame of reference to understand how.

The two of them looked at each other, and something passed between them. Gil knew that this man had died for him. He had died, not knowing that Carnhaina would bring him back to life.

"Time to talk," Brand said.

"Thank you," Gil answered. "We need to."

"Come, sit down then." Brand's gaze turned to the two Durlindraths, but it was Taingern who spoke.

"We'll wait outside, my friend."

Brand nodded. "Thank you. We'll not be long."

Gil pulled up a chair and Arell smiled at him. He saw worry in her eyes though, and he did not like it.

"You understand," Brand started, "that I had to pretend to be unwell. It was an opportunity to deceive Cardoroth's enemies, both those within the city and those without. But Ginsar, well, I don't think she'll fall for it. The nobles might."

"I understand," Gil said. "I should have realized it before now. Neither Shorty nor Taingern seemed overly worried. Did they know?"

"No, I didn't tell them. But they probably guessed. They've known me for a good while now, and understand how I think."

Arell poured Gil a glass of crushed juice, but she did not speak.

"My time in Cardoroth draws to an end," Brand told him. "I feel it in my bones. Everywhere I look, I see the signs. Soon, you will rule."

"I never wished it. I never wanted it. But I know that the responsibility is mine. I cannot pass it on to anyone else. It's a burden and an honor, and I hope that I'm up to it."

"You understand," Brand said. "And that pleases me. Even at your age you understand better than the nobles. They think that being king is all glory and wealth and triumph. They would learn a hard truth if their plots ever came to fruition."

"So they would."

Brand grinned at him. "They're mostly idiots. Never mind. We have more important things to discuss."

"Carnhaina's quest?"

"Indeed. And the seer."

"How do you know about the seer?"

"She saw me first, Gil. I knew what she would say to you. And it's true. There's a balance in all things. That is the key."

"Tell him," Arell said.

Gil saw the look on her face, and prepared himself for bad news.

Brand leaned forward in his chair. "The seer told me several things, but you don't need the gift of prophecy to see what will come next. War."

It was a bleak-sounding word, and one that sent a chill up Gil's spine.

"It's inevitable, then?" he asked.

"Yes. Ginsar, for all her thirst for revenge, for all her hatred of the both of us, serves a dark cause. There are those who would see Cardoroth topple, and all Alithoras

97

with it. They would rule the land themselves and bring with them a reign of blood and sorcery."

"And my quest?"

"It's doubly important. Cardoroth depends on it, and Alithoras needs Cardoroth."

"How shall I fulfill it?" Gil asked.

"You've started well," Brand answered. "You've begun as all quests must … by following your heart. But remember the advice of the seer. Balance is more inevitable than war, or peace, or life or death. It's the force at the heart of everything, for everything seeks balance and is always in motion to achieve it. It rules the world. Only people seek dominion and control to keep things just as they wish them. And of those who achieve it … it is a transient thing."

Gil looked at his mentor. "I don't know what that means. I don't understand."

Brand sighed. "There are times, Gil, when I talk like an old man. Never mind. What does it all mean? It's just how life works. And magic. And love. In all things there is a balance. Think of it this way. If you ran fast for a mile what would happen?"

"I'd get tired."

"Exactly. And what would you do?"

"I would rest."

"And if at another time you were sick and confined to bed for several days, what would you do when you were better?"

"I'd want to get out of my room, to walk around and see and do things again."

"That is balance, Gil. And what if you lifted a heavy object above your head?"

"Then I would have moved its weight above me."

"Yes. The object would be above you, but would you also not be exerting more force on the ground than before you lifted it? There are consequences to every deed, to every force."

Gil considered that. He thought he saw where Brand was leading him.

"Then if Ginsar has opened a gateway that should not have been opened, if she has allowed a force into the realm that should not be here, how would the world seek balance? Or how would the magics involved seek equilibrium?"

"How indeed," Brand said. "I don't know. But that's what you seek. And Carnhaina's diary is as good a place as any. Already, it has led you where you need to go – and the more you understand the better you'll be able to interpret her words."

"And what of you?" Gil asked.

A look of determination lit Brand's eyes. "I will lead Cardoroth to war. But not quite yet. And if we survive, then I shall leave. My homeland calls to me Gil, now more than ever."

"Cardoroth needs you," Gil said.

"Once, maybe. Now, perhaps. Later, there will be you. Lead her well, for the realm is grand and the people deserve a good future. You can give it to them."

"And if I'm not up to filling my grandfather's shoes? Or yours?"

"You won't know until you're in that situation. It will test you, but there's only one way to find out."

Gil thought very hard and very quickly. "If you wish," he offered, "I would renounce my claim to the throne and name you as king. I would do this not to avoid my responsibilities as I once would have, but to keep you here. I don't want to see you go where I can't follow."

Brand sat back and looked at him thoughtfully. "I appreciate that. You are ... you are like a son to me. But I have taught you well, and you are ready now to fulfill your destiny. Mine rests elsewhere, but that does not mean that we won't meet again."

Gil felt the ache of loss already. But he knew that what Brand said was true, and no matter the outcome of their conflict with Ginsar, there was great sadness ahead.

18. Light and Hope

It was dim in Carnhaina's study. Every time Gil came here, he produced light through the lòhrengai at his command, but it never seemed as bright as it did elsewhere. He wondered if there was some remnant of magic that lingered long after her death that subdued other powers.

It was an interesting thought. This was her place, her private study, a room where she must have worked countless acts of magic. It was here that she had written her diary, and there was magic of a kind in that also. But none of these things seemed as interesting just at the moment as Elrika. She sat on the desk before him, watching him patiently as he read the diary.

He looked up at her. She seemed as she always did, but there was a serious expression on her face and the sword that now hung at her side gave her a dangerous look.

"Keep reading," she said. "You haven't found anything yet, but the answers will be there, somewhere."

"I think I need a break," he said. "Let's talk for a bit."

"Alright, then. What do you want to talk about?"

"I don't know. Nothing. Anything."

"You're so, so *male* sometimes."

"You say it like it's a bad thing," he answered. "But really, I don't know what I want to talk about. But I like hearing your voice."

She gazed at him strangely for a moment. "Well, for someone who doesn't know what to talk about, you know exactly how to say the right things."

He smiled at her. "Maybe you just bring out the best in me."

"Now," she said, "now you're going too far. But I have something I want to talk about. Or at least that I want to ask you."

"What's that?"

"What really happened in that cave in the forest? There are rumors flying through the palace. It's said that Brand died, and Carnhaina brought him back to life."

Gil's memory of those events returned, sharp and clear. He knew they would remain that way, no matter if he lived for a hundred years.

"It's true," he said. "I saw it. And you should know this too. Brand is loyal to me and to Cardoroth. I know what some people thought, but he *is* loyal. He *did* die, and he died to save me." A sheen of tears came to his eyes as he spoke.

She reached out and touched his hand. "You don't have to talk about this if you don't want to."

He rubbed his eyes. "I think it might be good for me to talk about it. I feel so guilty. He gave his life to save mine, because Ginsar gave him a choice. Save his own, or save mine. And he chose me."

"He fought the Rider?" Elrika asked.

"He did. And he knew he could not win, but he fought anyway. And though he could not win, he managed to kill the Rider even as he died himself."

"And then Carnhaina came?"

"She came, and she saved him. Ginsar had left, knowing her greatest opponent was dead. And then

Carnhaina … I don't really know what she did or how she did it. It all happened so fast. But she said that because Ginsar in her madness had opened a gateway that should not have been opened, that it was possible. She said that the Horsemen come from another world, and that the walls of reality were sundered. She said that she had a chance to recall Brand's spirit and heal his body through the same way that Ginsar opened. And she did it. She returned Brand's spirit to his body, and healed his wounds."

Elrika stared at him. "Those were the rumors. It was hard to believe them, but I do now."

"It's all true, but it's also part of the problem. That's why the gateway has to be closed."

"Is Ginsar really mad? What was she like?"

"Mad?" Gil shivered. "She's insane. Worse, she's driven by a lust for revenge. One minute she's laughing, and then the next she fixes you with a stare that would freeze water. She's tall and beautiful, noble as a queen and dangerous as a snake in the grass."

"My, you can be quite descriptive!"

"Better a description than the real thing."

Elrika pursed her lips thoughtfully. "What do you think she plans now? You and Brand are still alive. That must infuriate her."

Gil stood up to stretch his legs. "Who can say? The next Rider will come, that's for sure. What will he do? I have no idea. Brand is preparing for war. That too is likely. I'm not sure what forces she has at her disposal, but there are elugs in the north and south of Alithoras. She must have some control over them, her and other elùgroths."

"I guess there are two wars really," Elrika said. "One will be a battle of swords. But the other is the important one. In the end, it won't matter who wins the first. The second, your quest, is the one that counts. If you can't close the gateway between worlds, then it's not just Cardoroth at stake, but all of Alithoras."

Gil sat down again. "You're right. And I'd better get back to this diary. Something in here will help. I'm sure of it."

He began to read again, flicking through the pages and looking for something of interest. As always, he had the feeling that the book showed him different things each time he looked at it, for he rarely seemed to see the same thing twice, but likewise he never seemed to reach its end. Magic. That's what it was. But it was of a kind beyond his understanding, and he wondered just how powerful Carnhaina had been. And why had she died after a normal span of life? The great masters lived longer than that. Aranloth, the greatest of the lòhrens, was said to be thousands of years old.

He kept turning the pages. Most of what he saw seemed to be random information. Some sections spoke of the balance of magic, but there was nothing there that he had not already discussed with Brand. One section was quite philosophical, and he read it out to Elrika.

"Light and Dark," Carnhaina had written. "Chaos and Order. Youth and Age. They are opposites, each on the furthest end of a spectrum. But only Man thinks of things in straight lines. In Nature, all is in motion. Everything goes through cycles, and one force leads to another. Thus it also is in human affairs, but the spans of our lives are too short to grasp this until age settles like a withering frost upon us. And this is worth considering. In the world, frost gives rise to spring again. Night transforms into day. But for Man, does Death lead to Rebirth? What a thought!

And one that the elderly mind is quick to ponder. But there are few answers, though I have learned some of them. But what use is knowledge? What will be will be, and the dreaded shall come to pass, as also the good in its turn. Yet these too are names given by Man. In Nature, there is neither good nor dread. There is just the Cycle. The wise man or woman, therefore, does not seek knowledge, but acceptance. For what good is knowledge without the grace to accede to the harmony of nature? It is a hard question, for it is a hard world. But the ancients learned this. The true leader waits. Inaction is a greater power than action, for action is the bluster of Man, trying to stamp his will on Nature. How foolish! How transitory! The wisest of leaders therefore does nothing, or almost nothing. But when they act, they act in accordance with the Cycle of Nature, and then all things are possible. So it is written, and thus has it proved to be during my long reign."

Gil closed the book. "She was a thinker," he said. "That's for sure."

"Did it make much sense to you?" Elrika asked.

"Not much," he admitted. "But I'll work on it."

Elrika slid off the desk. "Come for a walk then. We've been in here long enough."

Gil put the book down and stood. "I think you're right. There's a lot of what Carnhaina said bubbling away in my mind right now. Maybe a break will help something slip into place and I'll understand it better."

They left the hidden study and entered Brand's bedroom. There was still no sign of him, and Gil supposed that Brand intended to stay inconspicuous. This would help lull his enemies into a false sense of security.

105

"Is that where my sword came from?" Elrika pointed to the wall. There were weapons hanging there, but an empty space was visible where something had been taken.

"That's it. Lucky for me that in the old days they thought weapons made good decorations."

"You're trying to make light of it, Gil. But you had to fight for your life in here. I'm very proud of you."

He felt a thrill run through him at her words, but at the same time he remembered the desperation of that situation. No training could adequately prepare someone for something like that, and having gone through it he would never be the same again. But it also gave him an edge. He had faced that, and survived. His skills were good and his courage held up. It gave him confidence.

19. The Sword and Crown

They walked onward. Gil could not help but picture the dead Durlin that he had found on the floor. And the second one that was killed and hidden in a room outside. Those men had died trying to protect him, and a slow anger began to build. One of the perpetrators was dead, killed by Gil's own hand, but the second was free. That man *would* be found. And he would be brought to justice.

Outside the bedroom his current Durlin guards were there. This time, there were four of them and he thanked them for waiting. They seemed a bit surprised.

They fell in behind him and Elrika as they walked the corridor, their movements graceful and smooth as every Durlin's always were. Their presence was quiet and unobtrusive, but he knew how quick they could be if necessary. And he also knew that potentially another attack could come at any moment. His hand was never far from his sword hilt, and he noticed that Elrika's gaze was sharp and alert. Shorty and Taingern had made her a kind of bodyguard herself, and though that disturbed Gil, he also liked the fact that she was going to be spending a lot more time with him.

They had no particular destination, and walked for the pleasure of it and each other's company. Despite the enormous pressure of the situation and the prospect of difficult times ahead, Gil felt that all was right with the world. It was not a feeling that he was used to, and not one that made sense for him to feel now of all times, but it settled over him nevertheless. And he liked it.

Elrika paused as they came to a corridor that had a balcony.

"Shall we have a look?" she said.

Gil opened the door. It was cleverly crafted to slide on tiny wooden wheels that fitted within a groove made by a metal track. This allowed for a doorway that when opened did not restrict space in either the corridor or the balcony itself.

"Oh!" Elrika said. "I've never been out on one of the balconies before that was this high up in the palace."

They looked out over the balustrade. They were on the western side of the building, and Gil's gaze flickered first to the dark smudge on the horizon that was the forest. Ginsar was somewhere in those dark tracts of trees, plotting and scheming for his death and the destruction of Cardoroth.

Closer, he saw the length of the white road that scarred the chalky soil around Cardoroth City. It ran from the horizon to the West Gate, whose towers he could see rising up from the city wall, or the Cardurleth as it was often called. Attacking armies had marched the length of that road in the past, and the litter of sieges lay abandoned in the pastures to either side. Tall grasses grew green there, their roots seeking nourishment from the soil and the legions of enemy dead that rested below the surface. So Brand had told him, and in a dark way this gave him hope. Cardoroth had survived bleak times before. Many of them. And this would be no different.

Down below was one of the city squares. There were soldiers there, rank after rank of them, performing a drill with sword and shield. It seemed to Gil that everywhere he saw the signs of the future. War was coming.

The noon sun shone from above. The swords glinted dully, but brighter was the contrast of the paving. Each square tile was neatly set, and the city square offered a perfectly smooth surface for such practice, but every second tile was a shade of pale brown beside one of a far darker hue. Light glimmered from the first, but the second was like a murky puddle of water that absorbed all light.

It was an old square, repaired many times over the years, but like much in the inner city of Cardoroth, tradition kept it as it was at the time of the founding. Had Carnhaina once stood on this very balcony and looked down at soldiers drilling? She probably had, and it was a sobering thought. Soon, he would be responsible for the welfare of an entire nation, just as she had been. But he was no legend. Even so, he determined that he would see her proud of him.

"There!" Elrika pointed. "Is that Shorty?"

Two men stood apart, watching the soldiers drill. One was very tall, and he wore the crimson cape of a general. The other was certainly short, but it was too far away to tell if it was Shorty.

"If it's him, he's not wearing the white surcoat of the Durlin," Gil said.

"It's him. No doubt about it," Elrika said. "I can tell just from the way he's standing. Let's go and see him."

Gil was not sure, and he had no idea what made Elrika positive. Both men seemed to be standing the same way to him, but he was happy to take her word for it.

They closed the balcony door behind them, and moved quickly through the palace until they exited at a servants' door down on ground level. Here, the noise of the drilling soldiers was much louder, and the stomp of their boots on the tiles was a rush of determined noise that matched the single-minded expression on their faces. These men were new recruits, and they were training hard.

They skirted the square and came to the other side. Sure enough, it was Shorty. He saw them come, said something to the general and walked over to meet them.

"This lot has a way to go," he said, jerking his thumb toward the drilling soldiers. "But they'll get there."

"Drilling and fighting are different things," Gil said. "That's a lesson I learned recently. I guess they'll discover the same thing soon now."

Shorty gazed at the recruits thoughtfully. "Dark days are coming, true enough. But Cardoroth has seen such times before. Men such as these rise to the occasion. We all do. But it's true that drilling only takes you so far. A real fight is a different animal altogether. But tell me this, what else is drilling teaching them besides how to fight?"

Gil thought about that. It was true that fighting as a lone warrior was different than fighting as part of an army. But the essence of it all was the same. You had to defend against attack, and strike at your opponent's vulnerabilities. He knew that Shorty was trying to teach him something, but he could not see what it was.

"I'm not really sure," he answered. "It's teaching the men to trust in one another, to be part of a team."

"Aye lad, it's doing that. But it's also teaching them discipline. They learn to take orders from above. A simple thing, but they learn here to do it without question, and that adds *speed* to the process. In a battle, the ability to respond quickly to commands can make the difference between victory and defeat. When an opportunity comes, it must be taken. If not, the chance may be gone only moments later."

Gil thought about that. It was true. And it was a big difference from single combat. There was no chain of command there. No orders given and followed. It was lightening quick whereas an army was slow. Therefore, an army that was good at this, that became quick, held a decisive advantage.

"I get it now. I should have known that."

"You probably did. It would be in the books you study, but words on a page aren't real life. Some things you have to see to understand."

Shorty turned to Elrika. "Are you managing to keep him out of trouble?"

"I am. But who's going to keep *me* out of trouble?"

"A good answer!" Shorty laughed and winked at the Durlin guards. He looked again at the drilling soldiers. "This is thirsty work, standing out here in the sun. Let's say we get a drink. Have either of you palace-dwellers ever been to an inn before?"

They shook their heads, and Shorty grinned. "Well, let's fix that right now. There's a place close by that's friendly to soldiers. I've been there a time or two, and it's a nice place to spend a few hours."

He led them out of the square and down a few wide streets. Here and there a passerby recognized him and called out a greeting. Shorty responded to them all with a quick smile and a few words, though it became clear that they did not know him personally.

"Here it is," he said suddenly. "The *Sword and Crown Tavern*. Better known as just the *Sword*."

Gil saw the sign. It was a wooden panel hanging from two chains, and neatly painted upon it was the name Shorty had given and an image of a sword stuck into the ground at an angle. A golden crown perched at a rakish angle over the pommel, and a foaming mug of beer hooked by its handle on the sword hilt gave the impression of a drunk man standing there.

Shorty struck a similar pose to the image and Elrika giggled. Then he opened the door for them and they went through.

"I'll keep an eye on them," he said to the Durlin. "Best to wait out here so we don't draw attention to who they are. Sorry lads. No beer for you just yet!"

They went inside. It was neater than Gil had expected. Though the floor was made of timber it was covered by sawdust. This was to soak up spilled beer, or blood should a fight break out. At least so much Gil had picked up hearing soldiers talk. But neither seemed likely here. It was quite busy, but there were plenty of sturdy wooden tables and most folks were sitting down talking quietly with friends.

Shorty led them to an empty table and they sat down. A blonde waitress came over, her expression friendly.

"Welcome to the *Sword*. What can I get for you?"

"A tankard of beer for me," Shorty answered. "And I think perhaps two glasses of watered wine for my young friends."

The waitress turned to Gil and Elrika with a smile. "We have a fresh batch of white wine in. It's sweet and light, but don't drink too much. It has a harder kick than you'd think." She turned back to Shorty. "Anything to eat for lunch today?"

"Do you still make those meat pies here?"

"We surely do, sir. They're a crowd favorite and the cook has a batch just out of the oven now."

"Perfect," Shorty said. "Three of those thanks." He handed her some coins and she smiled and walked back to the bar.

"You're in for a treat," Shorty advised them. "Those meat pies are the best in the city. The beef is cooked nice and slow in a thick gravy, and the pastry is soft and buttery. They eat better here some days than at the palace."

Gil glanced at Elrika. He saw that she was excited, for she was being treated just as he was. Nor was this the sort of place that she was used to, and that added an element of interest. He was no more used to taverns than she was either, and that took his mind off his problems. He realized that perhaps it was for that exact purpose that Shorty had brought them here. For all his down-to-earth and ordinary ways, Shorty was one of the smartest and most intuitive men Gil had ever met. It was no surprise that Brand always spoke so highly of him.

The waitress brought over their drinks and gave Shorty some change. They drank quietly for a little while, savoring their surroundings. It was getting busier rapidly as more lunch-time patrons gathered. There were many waitresses now, all quick to clear used cutlery and bring fresh drinks. It was a well-run establishment, but when their pies arrived Gil's appreciation of the tavern increased further. Their aroma was fabulous and the taste even better.

Gil looked over at Elrika. Her father was the palace baker, but even she seemed impressed.

They finished their meal with little speech. All around them the conversations of the patrons grew louder, and were frequently punctuated by laughter.

Gil began to listen in to what was being said. Much of it was the ordinary talk of friends and family discussing everyday matters. But there was a darker undercurrent. He heard the word *war* repeated several times. There was discussion of Brand, and whether or not he was well, and if he would lead the army should some sort of attack against the city occur. Here and there, he heard the word *sorcery* as well. Though if this was in reference to Brand or the enemies of the city, he could not tell.

Gradually, a silence fell. It was strange after so much noise. People began to look out the tavern windows, and the three companions did so as well. They saw nothing, but there was a glimmer of light and a faint strand of music as though heard from far away. Something was happening, but Gil was not sure what. Yet it made him feel good somehow, and the talk of war and plots and the dark to come was momentarily forgotten.

20. A Flicker of Light

Night swept over Cardoroth.

The growing dark signaled the end of a shift for a company of soldiers stationed at the Harath Neben, the North Gate. This was what the people called Hunter's Gate, for the wild lands and woods beyond were rich in game. During the latter parts of the night, hunters would pass through regularly. There were the nobles and the wealthy looking for sport, or the poor and the downtrodden looking for cheap food. It was a boring time for the soldiers; they had seen it all before, and they had little interest in wild lands or in game. Better to be indoors, to find a lively inn where the beer flowed, the dice rolled and at least some of the female patrons were friendly – especially to those with coin.

Two soldiers, not really friends but sharing similar tastes, were headed away from the gate and walking an ill-lit street. It was in places like these that they found the entertainment they sought, and they were happy that for another week they were rostered for a day shift and the nights belonged to them.

"I heard a rumor the other day," one of them said. "Supposedly, Brand is dead."

"I heard that too," the second man replied. "It's not true though. One of my sister's friends works in the palace. She saw him return from the forest, all dirty and tired, but alive. And he brought back the prince with him. The Durlin were there too, and she says they were all covered in dust and grime."

"But," the first man insisted, "I heard the story from a sergeant who knows one of the Durlin themselves. He swore Brand was dead."

"Pah! Just stories. The city is always full of them. Few are true, and sergeants pass them on as readily as anyone else."

The first man considered that. "That might well be, but you have to admit that Brand is mixed up in some strange stuff. He's a warrior, but they say he's a lòhren too, a wielder of magic."

The second man laughed. "All those things, and king to be one day as well."

"No! Never that. He wouldn't do that to the young prince. Not that he couldn't if he had a mind to. But say what they will about him, Brand is loyal. He rescued that boy, didn't he?"

"That's true," the other said. "The real traitors are the nobles."

"Too right. That lot of troublemakers couldn't lie straight in bed at night, that's for sure. They're all crooked to the bone."

"Fools, the whole lot of them," the second man added. "They tried to usurp the throne themselves, and see where that got them? Brand has their measure. He's not a noble like them, and they hate his guts for it. But he's smarter than the whole bunch of them put together."

The first man hitched his sword belt a little higher, and felt for the hilt of the blade to be sure it was where it was supposed to be. This was just the sort of street where he may need it. When he was satisfied, he spoke again.

"The only problem with Brand is that he's too kindhearted. He should have killed the nobles aforehand. A noble with his head on a spike in the palace gardens doesn't plot much treason."

The other man laughed. "That's something we can agree on. Those nobles have it all coming to them. And Brand may yet have a chance to give it to them."

They turned a corner and entered a narrower street. It was silent and dark. They did not like it, and their conversation faltered. This was no time to get waylaid. It was payday, and their moneybags were full of coin. It was one thing to waste their wages on gambling and cheap beer, but another to lose it at the points of a robber-gang's swords.

A cold wind rose, picking up dust and litter before channeling it down the street ahead of them. Then suddenly the air warmed. There was a scent in it also, sweet and fragrant like a meadow full of flowers in the spring.

"Do you hear that?" the first man asked.

"Hear what?"

"Music. A strange, lilting music."

They stopped to listen.

"I can't hear anything," the second man said.

"It's gone now. I don't know what it was, but for just a moment I was home. I don't mean home here in the city. I mean where I grew up on a farm way out beyond the gate. I could almost see the hills about me, the sweet scent of pine and the memory of long, cold nights while the hearth burned. And my mother, at that same hearth cooking breakfast while the sun rose and sent streaks of silver through the frosted grass." He shook his head as though to clear it. "It was the darnedest thing to remember."

"Strange," the other man said. "I smelled the sea. My da was a fisherman. We lived way, way to the east. A tiny village it was. We came here when I was very young. Strange, I haven't thought of our old boat in years and years, but for a moment I felt it shifting under me."

The breeze died, and the dust and litter settled back down into place on the cobbled surface. But in the center of the street a shimmer of light briefly appeared before flickering away toward the corner and disappearing.

The two men looked at one another.

"What was that?"

"I don't know. But I feel different."

They paused for a moment, looking at each other as though embarrassed.

"I think I'll go home," the first man said.

The second looked down at the ground. "Me too. It's not a night to be out."

"See you tomorrow then. It'll be market day. That's always busy, but I think at lunch I'll go for a walk and buy my wife some of the perfume she likes."

The two men separated, one going back in the direction they had come from and the other forward. Both walked slowly, as though deep in thought.

Thrimgern pulled the great oak doors of his smithy closed. The day's work was done, and he was pleased. It was a profitable month, and the last order that he was working on was a big one.

It was a pity the order was for swords. At least he was able to charge a high price. The weapons were for a noble family, and prices were always inflated for them. His skill had something to do with it too. Not just any smith could make swords. Not quality ones anyway. But his best work, his love, was ornate doorknobs. Why did they not pay so well? The world was a strange place, but he would do what was needed to make his way in it.

Doorknobs. No, they weren't just doorknobs. They were the *best* doorknobs in Cardoroth. How he loved to craft them, to shape them out of a rough lump of metal, to transform them into the likeness of miniature animal heads that were so lifelike that people were hesitant to touch them for fear of being bitten. But the money was in *swords*.

No matter. He managed easily enough to pay the bills and keep his wife happy. She would be especially happy today when he told her about the price the noble family had agreed to pay. Or she would be happy once he had removed his leather apron and cleaned away the layers of soot and grime from his face and arms. The signs of a hard day's work to him – disgusting sloppiness to her.

He clipped the great lock into place through the heavy chain and secured the doors. Both lock and chain had been wrought by his grandfather many years ago. Strange that he should think of that now when he was so tired, but he had been there that day.

He remembered the chain being made, first by taking short iron rods heated to the working point, and then bending them back on themselves through a hole in the anvil. The rods were then hammered into a perfect loop over the anvil horn, red sparks flying from them. Many were made, and each two completed links were joined together by a third, this one bent and hammered through the others to form the link. And on it went until the great chain was fashioned. He looked at it now, and he could almost feel his grandfather there admiring the work as well, just as he had all those years ago.

Thrimgern smiled, lost in the memory, and then turned to walk to the house next door which was his home. Merril would nearly have dinner ready, and a glass of ale set down for him. She knew that smithying was thirsty work, and how much he enjoyed a quiet drink after a hard day of labor.

The front door was near when he felt a cooling breeze on his face. How sweet it was, easing away his tension and soothing his heat-reddened skin. He felt a change in the air, as though the weather was turning, and paused.

There was nobody in the street just now. But there was a light, a flickering light, and then momentarily he saw the slim figure of a woman, no a girl, young and fair. She smiled at him.

The sweat from his day's work stung his eyes. He rubbed them, but when he took his hands away she was gone.

It had been a long day. Wearily, he walked the last few paces to his home.

Grindar limped ahead, the grinding ache in his hip where the rheumatism often troubled him was bad tonight. That was the problem with getting old. All those aches and pains. And he was old as the hills and his body liked to let him know it. Still, he was able to light the street lamps and that kept food on the table. There were times when life had been worse.

He shuffled ahead, lifting up the protective dome of each lamp and lighting the candle wick. It was an easy enough job, but in truth he enjoyed still feeling useful.

The candle he was lighting flared to life, and the yellow light flickered over the leathery skin of his hands, all wrinkled like scrunched up parchment. At least he couldn't see his hair. That, he knew, was white and wispy. What was left of it, anyway. A far cry from the long raven-black hair he had once been proud of.

Time was nobody's friend, he mused, but what would be would be. It was not going to get him down. He shuffled ahead once more, his thin legs not much thicker than the poles upon which the lamps were set, but they got him around the city and that was enough.

He began to whistle as he walked. He did not care that no one else knew the tune. It was the price of getting older, but once that same tune had echoed through the streets about him. It was whistled. It was hummed. There were words that went with it too; merry words for merrier times. But they were all forgotten now, overwhelmed by the music of a different generation. No matter. *He* knew, and *he* remembered. That was enough.

He lit yet another candle, but just as the wick caught he saw a flicker of light from the corner of his eye. Turning, he saw a girl on the street behind him. What a vision she was! And just looking at her he felt younger. She was the most beautiful girl he had ever seen.

She smiled at him, and his heart fluttered in his chest. Her eyes seemed so bright, and her smile was like a summer's day, but there was sadness in her glance and the wisdom that came with deep sorrow. Oh, he knew that look, but he had never seen it on a girl like her before. She had seen a thing or two in her time, that was certain. But who was she?

She smiled again, and her face seemed to him brighter than the light from a thousand candles. Then she walked away, but before she turned the corner she looked back and their eyes met one last time. He felt a sudden stab of sorrow. She was too good for this world, and the good did not last.

She disappeared around the corner. He missed her already, but he felt a touch of youth course through his body, and there was strength in his limbs as he had not felt for many a year. Better still, his eyes saw clearly as they had not done for a very long time, and he whistled again for the sheer joy that bubbled up inside him.

He felt like he was young again, and he almost went to follow her, but his years had brought him not just white hair but a measure of wisdom too. No joy would come from chasing after the impossible.

121

With a sigh he walked ahead to the next lamp, a wistful smile on his face. That girl *was* too good for this world. But she would try to do good while she was here, that much he felt with certainty, but it could not last for long. Nothing ever did.

He went about his work, and his thoughts turned from the strange girl to his first and his only true sweetheart. Oh, that was very, very long ago. But he remembered her well.

21. The Oath

Gil, Elrika and Shorty made their way back to the palace. The Durlin guards trailed closely. No one said much, for it had been a strange afternoon and they were thoughtful.

Ahead, a troupe of singers came into view. They were dressed in flowing robes and ancient costumes. Their voices rose in unison, giving voice to an old ballad about a hero of the Camar before they came to Cardoroth. There was a piper with them, and the sound of his music rose sweetly into the air.

Gil and the others moved a little to the side to allow the troupe room to pass. One carried a cloth bag, and it was in this that listeners threw a coin if they liked what they heard. Shorty did so, but just as he reached out there was sudden movement from elsewhere in the line of singers.

One of the men, his cloak flowing behind him, detached from the group and lunged toward Gil. He was fast, and steel flashed in his hands. Shorty yelled and had begun to react, but Gil knew that he would not be able to intervene in time.

Gil reached for his sword, but he also would be too slow. They had been caught off-guard, and panic surged through him.

The assassin was close now, bridging the gap swiftly, and the dagger in his hand thrust forward in a deadly strike. But from near to Gil, Elrika moved. She was faster than them all. One moment her blade seemed poised in mid-air, and the next it darted forward in a deadly thrust.

Elrika's bodyweight was behind her thrust, even as they had both practiced so many times in the training yard, and the blade barely slowed as it slid through the attacker's clothing, through fat and muscle into the vital organs of his torso. And then, also as they had practiced, she angled the point of the blade upward at the end of the movement, and drove the tip behind the ribs and up toward the heart.

The man turned and twisted. With a grunt he staggered to the side and wrenched the blade from Elrika's grip. She cried out in surprise or pain, and the man that she had struck turned upon her.

He reached out with both hands, one still holding the dagger and the other clawing at the air. But he slowed and swayed where he stood, her sword still in his belly, and a froth of red blood at his lips. He tried to yell, but the blood flowed thicker in his mouth and he made only a horrible gurgling sound while red froth sprayed into the air.

Elrika held up her hands, but her face was spattered red. She stepped back, and the assassin fell to his knees. He fixed her with a stare of hatred, and then fell face forward to the ground. One leg kicked for a moment, and then he stilled.

The assassin's dagger lay dropped on the cobbles near the dead man's hand. Gil had seen its like before. It was a Duthenor blade. But now he knew that it was not at Brand's doing. These were Brand's enemies, enemies from his faraway homeland. They were still trying to mark Brand as a murderer. But why?

Gil turned to Elrika. She stood there, perfectly still. Her face was splattered with blood and her eyes were wide with fright. He reached out, intending to touch her shoulder, but she slumped against his body and hugged him fiercely.

"It's all right," Gil said. And he hugged her back.

The Durlin were all around them now, but there was no further threat. The singing troupe was in shock, and Gil knew they had nothing to do with it. The assassin had merely used them as cover to get close.

Shorty knelt by the body and examined it. Then he stood with something in his hand.

"We won't learn much from him. He's dressed in ordinary Cardoroth style, but the dagger is of Duthenor design. As is this."

He held up a brooch. It was of a snake looped in a circle and swallowing its own tail.

"I've never seen anything like it," Gil said.

"It's not a Camar motif. It, like the dagger, are of Duthenor design."

"They don't really care about me," Gil said. "All they want to do is get Brand in trouble, perhaps even executed as a traitor."

Shorty pocketed the brooch. "True enough."

"What shall we do about it?"

The Durlindrath scratched his head. "There's not much we can do. There's a vipers' nest of enemies somewhere in the city. But it's not our job to find them. We have other tasks. Sandy is looking for them, and we have to trust in her, and believe me – there's no secret she can't uncover given enough time."

"And then?"

"Then Brand will deal with them. Some at least are his countrymen, so it'll be fitting for him to decide their fate. He's their rightful chieftain, after all."

"No doubt," Gil answered. "But what then?"

"Ah, you have guessed. By sending these men the usurper who rules the Duthenor has woken Brand's dormant oath. He swore a long time ago to avenge his murdered parents and reclaim the chieftainship. That day is now fast approaching. Soon, he'll leave Cardoroth and the usurper will wish that he'd left Brand alone."

"Can Brand do it though?" He gestured to the body of the assassin. "He has enemies beyond just one usurper."

"Don't judge the Duthenor by what you've seen. These men serve the usurper, and may come from a neighboring tribe anyway. Most Duthenor are like Brand, and they would have him as their chieftain with great joy, if only they had the choice."

"But if he goes, he cannot leave as regent, nor take an army with him."

"No, he'll go as a lone warrior, even as he came to us years ago. Don't fear for him though. See what he achieved coming to Cardoroth? A lone barbarian from the wilderness? Now, he's a greater warrior than he was then, and a lòhren too. No, don't fear for him. Fear for his enemies!"

Shorty turned to Elrika, and the fierce expression on his face softened. "You did well, today. Very well. I'm proud of you."

Elrika nodded slowly, but did not answer him.

"We'll work on your wrist strength next. But for today, you've earned the right to walk proud among any group of warriors in the city." He hesitated, trying to assess her emotional state. "You did what you had to do, Elrika. And think on this. If you had not done so, Gil would be the one lying there on the ground now."

Elrika bit her lip and nodded once more, but still she did not speak.

They turned to go, the Durlin close all about them. Gil led Elrika forward, still holding her hand, and he saw Shorty mouth to him away from her sight. *Talk to her.*

He would do so. But he knew she was not ready just yet. For the moment, she just wanted to hold his hand

126

while she came to grips with what had happened. Then, she would want to talk.

He thought of the other things Shorty had said while they walked back to the palace. It was all true, and Gil had heard some of it himself from Brand's mouth. But one thing Shorty had not said. Would Brand really go alone? Certainly he would not take soldiers with him, or anything like that, but Gil had a feeling that he would not be *totally* alone.

22. Balance

It was late in the evening of the next day, and Gil sat with Elrika in Carnhaina's study once more. Here, where it was just the two of them, in this place of the palace that was theirs alone, she had opened up to him about killing the assassin.

"How is it," she had asked, "that I regret killing him even though it was necessary to save you?"

Gil had no easy answer for that. "I think that sometimes life forces things on us, gives us choices where there are no perfect outcomes. Had you not acted, I would have been killed and you would have felt guilty. If you attempted to disarm him, he may have killed us both because it was only by the decisive strike that you made that you got through his defenses. That man was committed to his cause. Neither a blow to arm or leg would have stopped him."

"I know Gil. I know, but I still feel bad. It was horrible."

He remembered the blood on her face and the look in her eye. Small wonder that she felt as she did. He was still grappling with the fact that he also had recently killed, and he had as yet found no answers for himself. But he understood just now how she felt, and perhaps it was enough to discuss it, to share their feelings and accept that there may be no answers to their questions.

They had talked for a good while. Then he had read from Carnhaina's diary. Once more they spoke, but there were no answers to any of their questions. But he felt the bond between them grow. They had been through a lot together, and their friendship was deeper, stronger, more enduring than it had been before.

"Have you heard the rumor going around the palace?" she asked him.

"Another one? What's Brand supposed to have done now?"

"Not Brand," she said. "And not just the palace. This one is about a girl."

Gil had in fact heard people in the palace talking about a girl.

"The beautiful one? The one with a light in her eyes that comes and then disappears?"

Elrika frowned at him. "You don't believe?" she asked.

"I don't know. There've been lots of rumors lately. None of them very close to the truth. Perhaps in these dark times people are searching for something good."

"Maybe," she said. "But this one feels different. And there are people, even here in the palace, who swear they have seen her themselves."

Gil had not heard that. But then people spoke to Elrika often. For the most part, he spent his days alone even though he was surrounded.

"Do you think it means something? Could it relate to something Ginsar has done? This girl doesn't sound at all like one of the Riders she's summoned though."

"No, I don't think it's anything to do with Ginsar. Not by the stories I've heard."

Gil leaned back and considered things. "Here's an idea," he said. "This girl appears about the same time as the Riders. But if she's nothing to do with Ginsar, who is she? I keep reading about balance and harmony. Brand has spoken of it. The seer talked about it. Is it possible that this girl came through the gate that Ginsar opened for the Riders? Has she come through with them, but is really their opposite?"

Elrika pursed her lips. She seemed to be thinking hard, but all she did was shake her head.

"Who can say? Maybe all that is possible. Maybe. But we just don't know. Nothing seems to be simple anymore."

Gil knew what she meant. Nothing had been simple for a while now, nor was that likely to change anytime soon.

"You're right. We just don't know. But that only means one thing."

She looked at him carefully, sensing the determination in his voice. "You're going to try to track her down?"

"Exactly," he said. "That will be the surest way of finding answers, one way or the other."

"Have you considered that it could be a trap?"

That surprised him. He had considered no such thing, but it was entirely possible.

"You're a pretty valuable person to have around," he said.

She winked at him, something that he thought she had picked up from Shorty, but it was a relief to see a lighthearted expression on her face.

"We'll have to be careful," he said. "But truly, I don't think this girl, if she even exists, is part of one of Ginsar's plots. I've seen one of her Riders in person, and the other in a vision. There are two more yet to come. I don't think she's one of them. She seems precisely the opposite, and the more I think on it the more I believe that she may have something to do with the balance that everyone keeps talking about."

"But you'll be careful anyway?"

"Of course. I've been wrong before, so I don't intend to take anything at face value."

Elrika seemed satisfied with that. "And how will you try to find her? It's a big city."

That was something that he had been thinking about. It would not be easy, but the first inkling of an idea began to form in his mind.

23. I've Found Them!

Brand sat on his accustomed chair next to the ornate throne of Cardoroth. Everything was the same as it always had been. The throne room. Cardoroth. The world. But *he* was different. He had died, however briefly, and nothing could be the same after that.

At one moment he thought how empty everything was, how futile. For all endeavors eventually failed, and all that lived became dust. The next, he appreciated the beauty of life, that each moment was golden and that there was joy in the simplest of things: sun on his face, a cold glass of water, the smile of a passing stranger. Both life and death seemed masks over the same thing, but his mind could not quite perceive the single face beneath.

"What are you thinking?" Taingern asked.

"Nothing. Everything. It does not matter."

Taingern raised an eyebrow, but he did not reply.

A Durlin opened the great door to the throne room and entered. "One of your counselors is here to see you, my lord."

Brand did not need to ask which one. He knew, for he saw the puzzlement on the guard's face. No one knew who this counselor was, what she did or how she did it. And that was the way it was supposed to be.

"Let her in," Brand said.

Sandy came through quickly. She was old, but she moved well and showed little sign of her age. Of course, Brand could not be sure exactly how old she was, for she kept her personal life private. The irony of this, given what she did for the realm, amused him.

She swept the room with her gaze, seemingly to ensure there was no one else there. Then she glanced behind her to check that the Durlin had left and closed the door. She offered no greeting nor any small talk. As always, she was straight to the point.

"I've found them."

Brand always liked her directness. Just now, he liked even more the news she brought. He did not have to ask who *they* were.

"Where?" he said simply.

"They're based close by – a house near the palace."

She gave no emphasis to those last words, but Brand intuited what she meant. It was a house of the nobles, the house of a traitor who would conspire, and hide, foreign assassins.

"How many are there?"

"Five," she said, holding up one hand.

"Will they be there tonight?"

"If they follow their normal routine, yes. But later. They drink a great deal, according to my informant."

Brand grinned. "The Duthenor are like that, sometimes. But even so, they may be good fighters. Are the traitor nobles with them?"

"No. I'm still looking for them."

Brand turned to Taingern, and the Durlindrath anticipated his wishes. "Not the city watch, then? You want some Durlin?"

"Yes. Ten of them, I think. You and Shorty shall lead them. Besides that, another ten soldiers – make them the best as recommended by the captains of the four gates. That way the whole city will be represented."

"And?"

Taingern knew what he was thinking, as he usually did. Brand grinned at him. "I'll be going too."

To his credit, Taingern did not try to dissuade him from that.

"Also," Brand added. "We'll go in plain clothes. No Durlin surcoats, no soldiers' uniforms. Tell the men this may be hard. The Duthenor will not go easily. And I want them, or at least some of them alive. I need answers."

"As you wish. What time shall we leave?"

"We'll assemble here, in the throne room. Make it the hour before midnight. It won't take long to get to this house, and the late hour should give the Duthenor time to grow tired and careless."

"They keep a good watch," Sandy said. "But they don't think they're discovered, and that will work in our favor."

By that, Brand knew, they were somewhat reckless. Sandy always understated things. But reckless Duthenor were dangerous. He should know, after all.

24. Who are You?

Gil knew what he was going to do, and there was no point in waiting. It was already late at night, but there were some things that could not be put off until the next day.

"I can seek out this girl," he told Elrika. "And I can do it with lòhrengai. At least, I can make the attempt."

They left Carnhaina's study, and the Durlin went with them. If they wondered what he was doing this late at night, they did not ask.

Up they went, right up to the top of one of the palace towers. It was a long climb, and Gil's legs burned. He noticed that neither Elrika nor the Durlin showed any sign of discomfort. That the Durlin were strong and fit was no surprise, but Elrika stuck with him every step of the way, and that impressed him. She had courage, she had skill with a blade and she evidently had endurance too. With the right training, what might she achieve? Small wonder that Shorty and Taingern were giving it to her.

They reached the top of the tower and walked out to the crenelated fortification that ringed the open circle at the top.

The dark was still and cool about them, the stars twinkling above in the late-night sky. Below, the city was a mass of shadows and bright-lit streets. Further away he saw the Tower of Halathgar. That was where Carnhaina had worked much of her magic, but he realized that she would have done so in lots of places, maybe even including where he stood now.

And magic he must work too, of a kind he had not attempted before. But the power was coming to him more easily of late. He felt confident, but not certain of the outcome.

They gave him a little space, and he stepped right up to the crenellations. Slowly, he composed himself. He breathed deeply of the air, drawing in the night, feeling the shimmering sky above him and the flickering city streets below. He became one with them, and he felt the lòhrengai within him flutter to life.

Down below there was movement. A group of men strode with purpose along a street, and one led them, his stride both swift and poised. That man seemed familiar to Gil, and at his thought the lòhrengai he had summoned leaped down to the city below. It was Brand. What was he doing? Where was he going this late at night?

Gil withdrew. He did not wish to disturb or distract the regent, which surely he would do if he probed any further with lòhrengai. Whatever questions Brand's presence late at night on the street below raised, they were questions for tomorrow. Right now Gil had a task to accomplish, and he felt a sense of growing urgency.

He cleared his mind, and opened himself to the pulse of the city below. His thought began to encompass it, reaching out all the way to the Cardurleth that circled the vast maze of streets and buildings and parks. At the same time, he sought his center, that place within himself that was the wellspring of peace and fear, hope and detachment, imagination and logic.

The marks on his palms tingled. All around him he felt acutely aware of life within the city, and he felt another kind of power also. This was one that he had not felt before, and it emanated from the dark sky. Each star, though incredibly remote, shimmered in his mind. And the constellation of Halathgar most of all. It was something that he had not experienced before, and was another sign that Brand had been right. The power within him grew as he used it rather than increased by being taught.

He accepted this new feeling, and then ignored it. His task now was simple, and he focused upon it. He reached back into his memory, recalling all that had been said of this girl that he sought, and then he cast those thoughts and images and feelings across the city. *Where are you? Come to me! Reveal yourself!*

All at once he felt something change. What he had expected, if it worked at all, was that he would sense her presence in some faraway part of the city, perhaps brush against her mind and get some understanding of who she was, where she was and what she was doing. But he got more than that.

The girl was very close by. And swiftly, almost as though she had been waiting for such a call from him, she came. There was a rush of light and a dazzlement of stars. He grew momentarily giddy, and then his mind cleared again.

"She comes!" he said, and he felt those around him stiffen in surprise.

And then she was there. She stood upon the very air beyond the parapet. Ephemeral. Beautiful. Remote. A sense of peace and goodwill radiated from her like warmth from the sun.

Gil suddenly thought of Brand. The regent and the girl were similar in some way that was not immediately apparent, but nevertheless striking.

137

"Who summons me?" she asked, and her voice was both light as a whisper and strong as steel.

Gil answered. "I have sought you out. I am—"

"I know who you are. I have read it in your eyes. You are more than you would say, but you don't know it yet."

Gil was at a loss. "What does that mean?"

"Time will show you. I see this, for I see what is, and what is yet to be."

"Who are you?"

"I? I am Life. And Trust. And Peace. I am also that which was before and will come after Time. You would call it Possibility."

This meant little to Gil. "But who *are* you?"

"I am your savior, and yet also, perhaps, your greatest sorrow."

"Lady. I'm confused. I really don't understand anything you're saying."

She gazed upon him, and there was a look in her eyes that may have been sorrow, but Gil could read her face no more than he could understand her words.

"Alas," she said. "You shall learn all soon enough."

"But—"

"No more!" She raised a slender arm before her to stop him. "There is not much time. Listen! I have been seeking you. Forces are loose in the world. They should not be. Not in *this* world. You must send them back whence they came."

"This I know," Gil answered, glad that what she said was at last clear. "I was charged with doing exactly that. But I don't know how."

The girl sighed, and it seemed that starlight shimmered through her body.

"You will learn. But you will wish that you had not. Yet first, you must know this."

25. Not in Cardoroth

Brand led the men. Gone was all pretense at being ill: he walked with purpose and acute watchfulness. His guise was no longer needed, though perhaps it had been fruitful. His enemies would not be expecting decisive action from him. Yet, wary as always, he was careful not to assume that it was so just because he wished it.

Even as he had ordered, there were ten Durlin and ten of the finest soldiers in Cardoroth. All were men of proven loyalty. He had briefed them personally when they had assembled in the throne room. He had told them to avoid bloodshed – if possible. But he warned them of the temperament of most Duthenor, and that the tribesmen were likely to fight no matter the odds against them. The men had merely looked at him, showing neither eagerness for trouble nor fear at its prospect. He was proud of them then, for they were *warriors*.

"Let's go," he had said. "Luck to us all."

Now, they walked through the streets of Cardoroth to the address Sandy had provided. It was not far, and he led them swiftly for he wanted no rumor of their march to proceed them.

His sword was belted at his side, as normal. But he carried something else. It was concealed within a sack and slung by a strap over his shoulder. If Taingern and Shorty knew what it was, they did not say. The men had no way of even guessing, and he sensed their curiosity. They would have to wait a little longer to find out what it was though.

They were nearly there. It felt good, even exhilarating, to lead men on a mission. He was not regent now, or at least so it felt. Nor was he a lòhren. He was … he was just a simple man as he had been years ago when he had first arrived in Cardoroth. Once, he had been a mere captain, and he envied himself that time in his life. The world was full of promise then. But no matter what he wished for, he could never go back to that. Or could he? It was an intriguing thought, but he brushed it aside. Now, he had a job to do. Thinking about the future could come later.

They turned a corner. The street they were now in was luxurious, even for the center of Cardoroth. A white wall marked the perimeter of a manor house. The grounds were large, but he could see little of them because of the wall. That was one of its purposes. It was also topped by intricately designed metal spikes to keep trespassers away. No matter. He did not intend to seek entry just yet. Sandy had given him a detailed description of the estate, and he had a vague memory of it himself. He had walked and ridden past it on occasion.

They came to a gate in the wall. There was one guard visible, but Sandy believed there was a second. The first was placed to watch for intruders, the second to seek help on any sign of trouble.

Brand was not going to do anything to give the impression trouble was coming. He led the men onward, and they had been warned not to look at the gate or show any sign of interest. Shorty began to sing, a bawdy song he had learned in a tavern long ago. To the guard, they would seem a mere band of revelers returning home.

There was a purpose in what they did though. Brand had eased back into the group. He was instantly recognizable, and he used the men around him to shield himself from view. He could have come by himself, hooded to disguise his face. But hoods were not commonly worn except in bad weather and he would have roused suspicion.

In the midst of the men, he fell in beside Taingern and Shorty who might also have been recognized. Quickly, Brand summoned lòhrengai, feeling it thrum through him. He let it drift out of his body and ease toward the guard. He sensed the first sitting in a chair in the shadows of the gate, and then he discovered the second. This one was stationed nearby in a little alcove in the wall. But there was a third with him.

Brand could not read minds, a talent that he sometimes wished to possess. But he allowed his lòhrengai to settle over the men. He sensed that the first guard was curious but not alarmed. The other men were simply bored. That was the feeling he worked with.

The men Brand led had walked past the gate now, and there was little time left. He took the feelings of boredom and intensified them. It was not a type of magic that he had attempted before, but all things were possible. He eased into their minds and gave them thoughts of sleep, of closing their eyes momentarily for just a few moments of rest. He thought of sleep rolling over them in a comforting wave, and of their tiredness because of their long hours of work.

His sense of the men faded as he walked further ahead.

"Did you do it?" Shorty asked.

Brand flashed him a grin. "They'll not hear us or see us now, but we'd better be quick. I don't think they'll sleep for long."

"That's a handy little trick."

Brand shrugged. "It's late at night and I think they had been drinking. I wouldn't want to try it during the day."

They continued on. The gate was now well behind them, swallowed up by the dark, and the white wall rose up close to their side. It was slightly different here though. This was an older section and not in as good repair. There were still metal spikes atop it though, even if not as well-made as the newer ones.

Brand gave a signal. The chosen soldier stepped forward and knelt before the wall. A second soldier, thin and agile, nimbly climbed up to stand on his shoulders. Slowly, the first stood.

From his high vantage point the second soldier drew out a short rope from beneath his cloak. Swiftly he tied this to the top portion of a metal stake. He let the end of the rope fall, and then quietly dropped down to the ground again.

Brand kept an eye on the street. There was no one coming either way. So far so good.

A group of men took hold of the rope and eased away the slack. Then carefully, they used their combined strength to pull. There was little noise. The metal stake began to bend, but then unexpectedly brick and mortar gave way.

There was a pop of dust, a grinding noise and then the stake broke free. It was more than what was intended, for bending it near flat would have done. Brand made to move, for he saw the metal stake flying through the air. If it clattered against the cobbles it would make enough noise to attract attention. But Taingern was closer. He had no chance of catching it, but he dived and speared out one arm before him. The bar struck it, and then bounced to the side. But when it hit the cobbles it made less noise than it otherwise would have.

Taingern rolled to his feet. Quickly, they went ahead with the rest of their plan. They were slightly slowed though, for the rope needed to be retied to the adjacent spike.

When this was done, they clambered up one at a time, slipped through the gap between spikes and dropped to the ground below. The last man drew up the rope behind him to hide it from sight, but he allowed it to dangle down over the inside of the wall. This was an escape route, if they needed one, but that was unlikely. Brand confidently took the lead again.

He wove a path through the manor grounds. Always he sought the deepest shadows, and ground that was maintained as well-clipped grass rather than garden beds where twigs or leaves could make noise beneath booted feet. This kind of stealth was not his talent, but he had done it before even if he did not have the skills of an army scout.

It was enough though. They moved through the grounds undetected. It did not seem to take long and they stood within the night-shadow of an oak grove looking out at the hulking shape of the manor house.

There Brand paused. He was not about to rush through the last hundred feet or so. It was all clear ground, and the possibility existed of being seen through windows. There was another risk too. Were the grounds patrolled? This was something that Sandy had not been able to discover.

Brand waited. The men waited silently behind him. No one moved. Everyone peered into the gloom, looking for signs of guards. There was nothing.

There was now no reason not to bridge the gap from their place of concealment to the house. Yet Brand still hesitated. He felt a sense of unease, but he did not know why. Yet, he had learned to trust his instincts.

He waited. They saw nothing. Slowly, he sensed the mood of the men around him change. *Why were they waiting?* He could give no answer. But a time came in any endeavor that a choice must be made: to proceed or to halt. He made his choice.

With a quick gesture he signaled it was time to move. He adjusted the sack that was slung over his shoulder, and then led the men forward. They did not run, for fast movement caught the eye. Instead, they walked slowly. And all the while they peered about them, looking for signs of guards or casual observers from the house. They saw nothing, but this did not still Brand's unease.

Brand did not like the feeling of being out in the open, no matter that it was dark. His hand strayed toward his sword hilt, but he did not touch it. The men would be looking at him as much as anywhere else, and if he showed signs of nervousness it would increase their own.

They reached the manor house without incident. There they gathered close to the deeper shadows of the wall to aid concealment. Nothing moved. Nothing stirred. All was silent. Yet even so, Brand did not like it.

There was nothing to be gained by prevarication. The confidence of the men would diminish though should Brand hesitate as he had before. Therefore, he went ahead straightaway with the plan he, Taingern and Shorty had developed.

145

Moving silently as a whisper, he eased himself along the wall, the men following him, until he neared a window. Carefully, he brought himself to a point where he could peer in from the bottom corner.

Now, he must be patient, and the men would understand that. He strained both eyes and ears to sense if anyone was in the room beyond. He did not think so. It was silent in there, and though he could see little there was no movement. To be sure, he summoned lòhrengai again, and let trailers of his thought drift into the room. Still, there was nothing.

Brand put the palm of his hand to the glass. He had explained to the men this part of the plan, and they had accepted he could do it. But he knew they were warriors and trusted in swords and steel more than magic. They would be uneasy with what he was about to do.

It did not matter. This was necessary to enter the house in silence, which was their aim. If they could surprise the conspirators within, bloodshed might be avoided.

He summoned the lòhrengai, and it blossomed in his palm. The glass was cold to touch, and he took that energy and concentrated it. Within moments the glass frosted up, strange patterns forming over it, swirls of white and silver that danced beneath his hand.

The glass was near to breaking, but if it did so it would shatter with noise. That was not what he wanted. He eased back a little, seeking now for something else.

There was harmony in all things. That was the balance of nature, and the seed of everything's opposite was contained within itself. He therefore sought out what warmth was left in the glass, and he drew it to his fingertips. There he gathered it, concentrated it, focused it in a small place.

146

With a sudden stab-like motion of his fingers, he released the heat in a surge. There was a pop, slight and barely audible. Several times he stabbed with his fingers and then a circular section of glass no bigger than his hand melted away and dripped down the glass.

A crack sprang through the rest of the frosted glass and Brand quickly cooled it. Then he waited a few moments, slowly withdrawing his power. The glass remained unbroken, but there was now a neat hole in it. He slipped his hand through and found the latch. Carefully, he lifted it and then eased the window open.

Brand felt the gazes of the men upon him. He did not like it, for he did not like to be different. Once, he was a warrior just as they, and distrusted magic. Now, he was a lòhren, and magic was another weapon at his disposal like knife, sword or bow. But the men, apart from Taingern and Shorty, were not likely to see it that way.

It did no good to think like that, and Brand shrugged the thoughts aside. He drew his sword, and nimbly went through the window into the dark. The men followed him.

26. Mother of Stars

Gil watched as the girl stepped forward. One moment she was in the air before him, and the next she stood upon the fortification before lightly jumping down to the flagstone base of the parapet.

It was a strange sight, and Gil wondered what powers she possessed. All the more so, because while she had seemed ethereal before now she was as solid as he was. She was real and not a vision. The night-breeze ruffled her white gown, and he could smell the scent of her hair.

He looked at her in wonderment. When she stepped close to speak to him her voice was soft but resonant, and he felt the warmth of her body even from a pace away.

"One is here," she stated. "One of the Horsemen. His name is Betrayal. But pay no heed to names. They are mere noises in the wind, for Death was Betrayal too. And Betrayal can be Death. The power of the Horsemen is not in their names. Nevertheless, Betrayal is in this city. Close. Very close."

Gil had a sinking feeling in his stomach. Elrika shuffled beside him.

"Where?" he asked.

The girl's arm stretched out, slim and toned, left bare to the shoulder by her white gown. Her eyes glittered with determination, but there was sorrow behind them too, even if hidden, and Gil saw it and wondered why.

"Behold!" she said with force. "Though the four Riders came before me I must follow, for the Mother of Stars seeks always for balance. Last I came, not summoned but drawn, and my powers still grow. Down there waits one of the Riders, and the man who defeated Death goes thither, but he does not know why. It is a trap, and he will die. This time, the true death."

Gil did not hesitate. "Not if I can help it!"

He knew what man she spoke of. Brand! And he had seen where the regent had gone. At least, he knew roughly, and the girl had said he was close, so he would not be hard to find.

He ran, and Erika and the Durlin ran also. They had heard the warning, and they intended to do something about it just as he did.

Down through the palace they raced, and the strange girl was with them. Who she was, or what, Gil did not care at the moment. All that mattered was reaching Brand and helping him. But nevertheless he knew that there was much more about her to learn, and that she had spoken only a little of all that she could tell.

The long corridors swept them by: doors, wall-hangings, startled servants all left behind in a dazzling rush. Gil raced as close as he could to a full sprint. Brand had been there when he needed him most. He *must* be there to return the favor.

Gil was fast. He had always been fast, and he led the others. The Durlin were close behind him, and just behind them he heard the separate footfalls of Elrika and the girl. That they kept up surprised him, but Elrika was full of surprises. He was not sure he *wanted* her to keep up though. Where they were headed was going to be dangerous.

They burst through the front door of the palace, and hurtled out into the gardens. Now, they could really run,

149

free of constraints and corners and a slippery surface beneath their boots.

Gil increased his pace, though his breath was already coming in great heaves of his chest. *Please! Please!* He thought as his feet pounded the ground. *Let me reach Brand in time!*

27. Neither Sword nor Helm

It was dark in the room that Brand and his men had entered. Dark and silent, for nowhere they heard any noise nor indication of anyone's presence. Yet Sandy had assured them that the conspirators they sought were here. This should have been pleasing, because it meant they slept, yet it only stirred Brand's sense of unease all the more.

One thing was visible though: a dim light ahead. Brand took it to be coming from an inner courtyard of the house. He had been told that one existed, and it seemed a likely place for the Duthenor to gather and share a drink. Such was the custom in Cardoroth. But if there was a light, where were the men? They would not leave a lantern burning for no purpose. Yet if they were there, sharing a drink, why could he not hear their talk?

Brand did not like it. But there was no going back now. He had come to find these renegade Duthenor, these conspirators that had tried to kill Gil and who sought to bring him down, and that he would do.

He moved ahead, one small step at a time, and the men followed his lead. He tried to remember what he could of houses such as these. Most rooms would border the inner courtyard. The center of the house was a paved and gardened area, often open to the sky. It was the heart of the house, where all occupants could gather in private and away from the hustle of the city. Here they would regularly eat, drink, tell stories or just talk. Often there were fruit trees in pots and vegetables as well as intricate ornamental gardens that looked tranquil and beautiful through the day but whose flowers released a range of perfumes at night. They were beautiful places, but not tonight. Tonight, every shadow was potential death.

Brand made a choice. There were many rooms in the house, but it made sense to head for the light first. That was where people were likely to be. So, he kept going in the direction he was headed, one slow step at a time, sensing the men behind him doing the same.

If he wanted to, he could cast out tendrils of lòhrengai to test where the occupants of the house were in the same way that he had done on the street with the guards. But that worked better out in the open. In a building, where there were likely to be several people all in fairly close proximity, it would not work well. Anyway, he preferred to do things the simple way, the way he had for most of his life.

He passed out of the first room and into a corridor. This, he did not like, for the men would be strung out and it would be difficult to bring their weapons to bear if that was necessary. But he could see the tiles of the courtyard ahead now, and that meant they were close to their destination.

Brand eased ahead, moving even more carefully now. The corridor gave way to the courtyard, and he felt space open up around him and a greater movement of air. The light was coming from the other side, perhaps forty or fifty paces away, and it was too dim to see much. The garden beds and tables and benches did not help.

He kept going, and he sensed the men behind him leave the corridor also and begin to spread out. They would be ready now for whatever was to come.

Beneath his boots were intricately decorated tiles. They were of varicolored geometrical designs, typical of such a house. There would be frescos on the walls as well, but all he could see of these were vague glints of color in the shadows. And there were too many of those. The courtyard was large, the shadows were thick and the conspirators could be anywhere. And still there was no noise nor sense of life within the house.

He paused then, uncertain as to what to do. This was not like him, and that worried him also. But his instincts flared to life. Something was wrong, and he had not survived the troubles of his past by ignoring his gut feelings. But what to do about them?

He felt the unease of the men behind him. Twice now he had come to a halt for no reason that they could see. Shorty and Taingern trusted him implicitly. The Durlin also. It was the soldiers that worried him the most. Whatever was done here would spread around the city. He could not afford to appear hesitant or undecided. Even worse, he could not appear to lack courage. These were fatal flaws in a leader, and soon, very soon now if he was not mistaken, Cardoroth would need a leader to guide them through battle and war.

Brand drew his sword. It slid slowly, almost silently out of its sheath. The hilt felt good in his hands, and the balance of the Halathrin-wrought blade was marvelous to feel.

The sword had been his father's, and before that belonged to a long line of Duthenor chieftains. The thought of all those ancestors, their blood in his veins, gave him a surge of pride. They were all dead now, but their names lived on. If he had come here only to die, then he would not go without a fight. He would leave a name after him fit to be spoken alongside that of his ancestors.

The blade glimmered palely before him, picking up the dim light from the other side of the courtyard. Behind him, he heard the whisper of many other blades being drawn.

Brand stepped ahead. He was ready now for what would come next, and he knew it would not be pleasant. But he would not be surprised. Nor would the men he led. If nothing else, his momentary hesitation had made them nervous, and nervous men were wary.

The light grew brighter. It flickered and shimmered, and Brand realized it came from a hearth. In many courtyards such as this, feasts were cooked out in the open when the weather was good. Afterwards, the household would gather by the dying embers to sip wine and talk.

He drew closer. The light flickered and flared, and he smelled the smoke now as the breeze changed direction. A moment later the light steadied, smoke drifted a little to the side, and a man was revealed.

The figure stood still, waiting. His pose was casual, yet he looked poised and ready to move in a heartbeat. That alone signaled he was a warrior, and the long sword at his side served only as confirmation.

Brand did not move. There was no need yet, nor was he about to go running into something that he did not understand. The man had seen him and was not surprised. He knew that men had come into his house to arrest him, for he was undoubtedly one of the Duthenor conspirators. It was obvious by the way he stood and the way he wore his sword, if not by his tall frame and pale hair. Yet why was he not surprised? Had he heard them

154

approach? Or had he somehow learned of the raid in advance?

The mysterious figure stirred. "We meet at last, Brand. Outlaw and hunted man."

The words did not disturb Brand. He would expect as much from one of the usurper's servants. But the situation *did* disturb him. Greatly. There was something terribly wrong about all of this, but he did not yet know what.

"Well met," Brand answered. "Thrall of a usurper."

The man merely shrugged. "I'm not that. No more than you're a typical outlaw. But this much is true. You're a hunted man, and have been for many long years. But the hunt is up. Did you ever think the king would forgive you for what you did?"

Brand remembered slipping into the usurper's house as a mere youth, the house that had been his own father's and that he had grown up in, and taking back his father's sword while the usurper slept.

"A king, is he? The title of chieftain is no longer enough, then?"

"It never was. But the time for words has passed. You will die now, as surely as you should have died all those years ago."

The man gestured. Out of the shadows behind him stepped the remaining Duthenor. There were only a few of them, but they looked like hard men used to fighting and confident of winning.

Their leader spoke again. But Brand searched the shadows with his gaze. The Duthenor were badly outnumbered. But they showed no fear. Why?

"You will die now, Duthenor that was and chieftain that never could be. And the hope that you sparked to life long ago back at home, the very hope that people carry in their hearts because you yet live, will die with you. And the rebellious spirit that they show, thinking that one day you might return, will wither to ash and dust."

Brand considered those words. They were true. Yet the opposite was also true. How greatly the usurper would fear the rise of the Duthenor if the rightful heir returned, not as the youth that long ago escaped the hunt, but as a grown man ready and able to fight.

"If just my life gave them hope," Brand said, "then imagine what they will do when I return to my homeland, as one day soon I shall."

Slowly, Brand reached into the hessian pouch that he carried slung over his shoulder. He dropped the bag, and revealed its contents. In his hand he held a helm. This he placed upon his head. Long it had been since last he wore it, but it fitted well and pride surged again within him. It gleamed with a silver light amid the shadowy courtyard, and the patterns etched within the metal caught the ruddy light of the fire and cast it back like the promise of blood yet to flow.

Brand straightened to his full height. He looked into the eyes of the leader who stood opposite him. For the first time, he read doubt there.

The Duthenor the man led seemed uneasy also. They shifted nervously on their feet, peering at this new development.

"The Helm of the Duthenor!" one hissed.

"Indeed it is," Brand said. "The mark of the Duthenor chieftains of old, and worn only by the rightful chieftain. And that is me. And I will reclaim what is mine, and the master you all serve shall be thrown from the hall that he stole, the hall in which he murdered my parents. This I have sworn, and I swear again that it shall be so."

There was silence. Doubt grew among the enemy, and Brand sensed his own men ready themselves for a fight. But that would not come yet.

The enemy leader regained his composure. "A pretty trinket. And I will not dispute that it is the real helm. How ever did you come by it? It has been lost to our people for hundreds of years."

Brand smiled. "A pretty trinket? A cheap name for something crafted by the immortal Halathrin and worth more than all the gold in this city."

"How then did you acquire it?"

"I was willing to pay the greatest price of all."

"And what was that?"

"My life," Brand said.

The man smiled at him. "I see that you did not make good your end of the deal though."

"It was close, but I bargained better than the seller expected." Brand raised the tip of his sword. "It was not easy."

"And who was the seller?"

"You have heard of him. Shurilgar the Sorcerer. Shurilgar the Betrayer of Nations."

There was silence again. Brand did not mind talking, for all the while he was trying to work out what else was in the shadows behind his enemies.

"That is a lie," the Duthenor leader said at last. "Shurilgar is dead. All men know it."

"I don't lie," Brand said. "Shurilgar is dead, but yet still his spirit endures in Alithoras. And it is dangerous beyond your reckoning. So, enough of this. Fight, or give yourselves up."

The man seemed disturbed. This was all more than he had bargained for, and he must have sensed the men

157

behind him wavering. But he had a surprise of his own prepared, and decided to play it now.

"You defeated a legendary opponent, if a dead one, to claim the helm. But," he said, allowing a note of triumph into his voice, "neither sword nor helm will save you from this!"

The man gestured toward the shadows behind him. "Come forth!"

In the darkness, there was movement. A figure began to take form as it came forward. Brand's heart sank. He knew that the Duthenor had some last card yet to play, but he had not expected this. But he should have.

There was a clatter of hooves. The figure was mounted, and a sense of menace came with it. It was one of the Riders. His steed was gray, its hooves shod by iron that echoed dully from the four walls of the courtyard. It snorted, and its ears flicked in agitation.

The Rider upon him seemed a tottery old man. His back was hunched, his eyes were red and rheumy. There was palsy in his gnarled hands, and the skin that covered them was thin, hanging in flaps from little more than bone. Yet there was power in his gaze, power that took the breath away.

Brand sensed the blood magic that formed the Rider, and his instincts as a lòhren flared to life. The uneasiness that had long gripped him was finally given visible form, and yet something was still wrong. Carnhaina had said the second Rider would be War. Yet this, surely, was Time. But Brand had no leisure to consider such things.

The horse came to a standstill, only its ears still moving. Its eyes were bleak pools of shadow that no light seemed to bring to life. The Rider upon him bore no weapon, but his rheumy gaze gleamed with fierce malevolence.

158

"Well met, Brand," the Rider croaked. His voice was soft, but horrible to hear. It was like a whisper coming up from the deep soil of a grave.

Brand lifted high his sword. "You do not belong here. Go back whence you came!"

The ancient figure laughed. His lips drew back tightly, exposing rotting teeth and blackened gums pockmarked with sores.

"Fool. I belong everywhere. And with you especially. I have been with you all the days of your life."

Brand forced himself to step forward. His Halathrin-wrought blade rose higher still. The fire in the hearth had burned to low embers, and the room was colored by its ruddy light. The smell of smoke was stronger now, for the breeze had stilled.

Time sat astride his mount and watched Brand with an expression of infinite patience. Then he shook his head.

"A fool until the end. You cannot defeat me. All men succumb to me, in time."

"Then I shall give you none!"

Brand leaped forward. The Rider's head wobbled on his neck, and a tremor ran through one arm. But his rheumy eyes narrowed and gleamed.

Brand stumbled and fell. His sword clattered to the floor, and the Helm of the Duthenor rolled from his head.

There was a momentary silence. Taingern stepped forward. Shorty came with him.

"And do you also seek the same fate?"

The two Durlindraths did not falter. "Where Brand goes, we go," Taingern said.

They continued forward. Nothing happened until they reached Brand. From there, they prepared themselves to attack, but just as Brand had been struck down, so were they. They fell as though struck by an invisible force.

The soft laugh of the Rider filled the room.

28. Now is the Time

Gil ran as he had never run before. The others were still with him. It had been a mad rush through the streets, and though not far their speed had been great. But there was a price paid for speed: they were already tired and he knew a fight was yet to come.

He halted suddenly. There he stood upon the dark street, for his senses had caught what he was looking for. In moments, the others caught up. He spared them a quick glance. Would they be enough for what was to come? The four Durlin were skilled in combat, and equal to at least double their number of ordinary warriors. Elrika was skilled as well, and she had no lack of courage. The strange girl, the only one of them seemingly unruffled by the run, stood there and gazed at him. She was a mystery too deep for him to fathom, and he had no idea of what she might be capable. That she was here to help seemed plain enough, but the manner of that help was something that he would only discover when it was needed.

"Where's Brand?" Elrika asked.

Gil did not answer. He had sensed the regent's presence, or rather the feel of his lòhrengai. Gil summoned his own. It came in a swift rush, flowing up through him and pouring out with a life of its own. The magic was getting stronger each time he summoned it, and Gil was not sure that was a good thing.

Straightaway, the lòhrengai speared with a blue light toward a gate set within a perimeter wall of a noble's mansion. Gil sensed something of what Brand had done

161

here. It was a small magic, but more subtle than anything that Gil could do. The traces of it lingered, and then further away, somewhere within the grounds of the manor, he sensed Brand's power again. This he could identify: heat and cold, the basic forces that lòhrengai often took and manipulated.

Gil thrust his hand out and pointed to the gate. "In there!" he cried.

The Durlin were quicker than he was. They raced to the gate and wrenched it open. There was a guard there in a chair, and he rose as the gate clanged. The man drew his sword and yelled. Gil heard footsteps pound toward them.

"Stand aside!" ordered one of the Durlin.

"Get out!" shout the guard in reply. The man wove his sword before him and the other two guards drew theirs with a hiss, their blades leaping into their hands.

Gil stepped forward. "I'm Prince Gilcarist. Do you recognize me? Brand is inside, and I'm going to see him. Whatever your orders are, I now revoke them. Stand aside!"

The guard studied him. "I know who you are, princeling. But I don't care. My master said not to let anyone in, and that's an end to it. Be off with you."

Gil felt anger rise. These men were not Duthenor, but Camar. But their lord was one of the nobles, no doubt one who plotted for the throne, Gil's throne, and the attitude of the nobles flowed down to their men. Yet still, he did not wish to see them harmed. But matters were taken out of his control.

"You've been instructed by your prince to stand aside," the Durlin spoke again. "Do it, or die. There is no more time to talk."

The guard spat. "That's what I think of you and the prince. Be off with you!"

The Durlin did not hesitate. There were four of them and only three guards. The guards did not have a chance, but probably did not even realize it. They had never seen the Durlin in action, but Gil had. His stomach churned with the thought of the violence about to be unleashed.

Without hesitation the Durlin acted. Their swords hissed from their sheaths and they bridged the gap between themselves and the guards with astonishing speed. Steel struck steel, but it was not a fight.

The Durlin were swift and skilled, while the guards were only average fighters. But the Durlin did not kill. Within moments they had disarmed the guards, sending their swords flying. One man fell to his knees, blood spurting from his hand, and the other two men backed away. But although the Durlin did not kill, they were not prepared to leave enemies behind them. The kneeling guard was struck with the pommel of a sword to his head. He collapsed like a toppled tree. The other two suffered a swift succession of kicks and elbows to body and head. They fell to the ground and did not move.

Gil was amazed. He knew the skill the Durlin had, but he also knew their rule. If ever they were forced to draw a blade, they must be prepared to kill. There was no safe way to merely try to disarm someone, but still they had risked it. They were good men, and their skill was only a part of it.

They sheathed their swords. "Let's go!"

This time, Gil and the others followed the Durlin. They knew where Brand was now, for the house was visible ahead through the night-time shadows. It hulked against the horizon, dark and forbidding.

Gil followed swiftly, wondering what lay ahead. He had no doubt the Durlin could deal with any physical threat, but there was likely to be magic also. And if Brand was in danger, then that magic would be very great. The question that ran through Gil's mind even as he raced ahead was what could *he* do to help?

The manor grounds were dark. Many of the nobles' homes had lanterns set on poles along the carriageway that led to the building. That was not so here, although Gil soon saw the poles existed but no lanterns were lit. He wondered whose house this was, and why Brand had come here with many men. The answer that came to him was one that he did not like. Sandy had discovered the hideout of either the rebel nobles or the Duthenor assassins.

They sped down the driveway. It was constructed of gravel to ensure that carriage wheels did not bog in wet weather. This meant that as they ran the sound they made was loud. But the Durlin made no attempt to move off the gravel, and Gil understood why. Brand may have come here in secrecy, but what mattered now was speed. Away from the driveway, there were gardens that would slow them down.

The house loomed ahead of them. They were close now, but the place seemed dark and quiet. No lights showed, and it seemed as though no one was even home.

Gil sent out tendrils of lòhrengai, seeking sign of Brand again. Perhaps he was not in the house but somewhere in the grounds. His mind swept the area, and his gaze also. He sensed nothing with the magic and saw only the shadowy outlines of trees and bushes and an expanse of well-clipped lawns.

He turned his magic toward the house. It was dark, relieved only by beds of bushes with night-scented blossoms that shone silver-white in the dim light.

The gardens would be beautiful by day, and the house also. And yet with a sudden stab Gil sensed evil within. Something was there, and it had summoned magic of its own. It was the Rider the girl had warned of, and Brand was already there.

"Hurry!" Gil shouted.

They had come now to the very front of the house. The gravel carriageway turned toward stables and sheds to the side. But a tiled path led straight to the front door. This the Durlin took, and the others followed close behind.

They came to a door set within a marble portico. The Durlin tried to open it, but it was locked. There was no way to force it, for it was made of solid oak.

One of the Durlin thought of something. He went swiftly to one of the nearby gardens and lifted up a large rock from the line of them that formed an edge to a flower bed. This he brought back and flung into the window of the room next to the door. There was a shrieking clatter of ruined glass and shards flew everywhere. He stepped forward then, his sword drawn, and kicked in the remaining glass.

"Careful!" he warned as he stepped through into the house.

The other Durlin were close behind. Gil stepped through next, followed by Elrika and the strange girl. It was dark inside, and Gil drew his sword also.

It was quiet again after the sudden noise. There was no movement nor sign of life. For all that Gil wanted to race ahead and find Brand, now was no time to be hasty. He could not help the regent if he were killed in the attempt. So, he followed the lead of the Durlin, who were far more experienced than he was.

The Durlin fanned out. Three went slowly ahead, swords drawn and creeping forward step by agonizing step. The fourth formed a rearguard.

Gil went forward with Elrika beside him. He could see her face in the dim light: pale, scared but determined. She may not yet have the skill of a Durlin, but one day he knew she would. She was gifted. And if she did not have that skill now, she was still dangerous. He would not like to cross swords with her.

The strange girl was just a little to his side and behind him. Could he trust her? He had no way of knowing, but his instincts told him that he could. She seemed to move without sound or fear, nor did she carry any weapon that he could see. For all that she had first appeared as an ethereal vision, she was solid now and there was no sign that that was going to change. Perhaps, even as she had said, she was seeking him, and having found him she would now remain with him. Perhaps, having become flesh and blood, she could not return to her former state.

The Durlin led them out of the room and into a corridor. This was not wide, and they drew close together. Gil could tell they did not like it. If they were attacked, they had no room to maneuver. As a consequence, their pace quickened.

Within moments a dim light showed at the end of the passage. It was faint, and the smell of smoke was in the air. Gil did not like that. Was the house on fire? He realized though that this was not the case. The corridor was headed toward a courtyard. It was natural that a fire would be set there in a hearth, and it explained the light also.

The Durlin paused. They had heard something, and then Gil heard it too. Voices.

There was nothing to do besides go forward, and this the Durlin did. Their white surcoats made them more visible in the dark, but that could not be helped. If they were worried about arrows or daggers flung from the dark, they did not show it. The possibility would have occurred to them though, and this was why they now held their blades vertically in front of their bodies. This position increased the surface area of the weapon before them, protecting them a little more than if the blade were held point forward. Brand had taught him that once, but he had forgotten.

Gil raised his sword in the same way. Slowly, the courtyard emerged into his view. There were figures there waiting for them. He could make little out except that there were two groups and that the presence of evil that he had sensed before suddenly increased.

In a few more paces he saw what he had wished never to see again. Brand was there, but the regent was on his knees. Shorty and Taingern lay stricken beside him. And beyond, now visible, was the nightmare figure of a Rider. It was not the one the scry basin had shown him, but the jolt of the creature's presence rocked him. It did not matter which it was, for each was as bad as the other. Each was a blight upon the earth, a presence in this world that should not be here and that sought the destruction of all that he held dear.

Gil gritted his teeth. One thing was certain: Brand was not dead, and he had arrived in time to help. But what could he, or the Durlin, do that Brand and his men had not already tried?

Through the shadowy light Gil sensed the eyes of the Horseman upon him. He looked up and held that awful gaze. But the evil that he sensed before was as nothing. Now, he felt a wave of hatred wash over him like a withering wind.

He understood how Brand and the Durlindraths had been felled. There was magic in the air, and Gil was only on the outer edge of it. Closer, he sensed that the force was stronger by far. There was hope in that too, for strong as this magic was, it had limits. And distance was one. But that thought was not overly comforting. He could not hope to defeat the Rider without getting close. But if Brand had fallen, how could he, so much lesser in the powers of body and magic, expect to approach and take the fight to the enemy?

Gil tore his eyes away from the Horseman, and the sense of being overpowered reduced. He glanced at his companions. They were rooted to the spot as was he, unable to move.

But one figure did move. Brand reached forth with a trembling hand and gripped the hilt of his sword that lay on the tiles before him. Slowly, he rose until he stood upon trembling legs. There he swayed, a picture of defiance in the face of all odds.

The Rider spoke, and his ancient voice was a croak of amusement.

"Ah, but this is glorious. So few, so very few defy me. But listen, mortal, and understand. None defy me for long."

Brand did not answer. He took a tottering step forward. But even as he did so Gil saw that it made him weaker. It confirmed that the magic of the Rider was stronger the closer it was brought to bear.

The Duthenor around the Rider laughed. Brand responded to this with a mighty effort, standing straighter and taking yet another step. But his arm that carried the sword trembled as though the blade were made of lead instead of Halathrin steel.

Gil was amazed. There was no give in Brand, and he would fight to the end. But this did not appear to be a battle he could win. He had not found a weakness in the enemy's power to exploit. Nor could Gil see one either. What arrogance had driven him to come here? He could not help. He was powerless. And yet he *must* find a way. For Brand, he would do anything.

The tribesmen taunted the regent. "Go ahead," they said. "Move closer. Each step is death, and we shall tell the tale of your fall at home. Every Duthenor, young or old, will hear it. We shall tell how you fell, how you died, helpless before your enemy."

Brand glanced at them. His gaze was colder than ice, and they fell silent.

He turned his eyes back to the Rider.

"Come, face me then. If I cannot walk to you, walk to me."

The Rider studied him a moment, as though assessing if he were capable of any harm. Then he nudged his horse forward, and a new wave of malice filled the room. It smashed into Gil like a wave, and he crumbled to his knees.

But somehow, despite it all, Brand remained standing. The Rider dismounted, his frail-seeming figure all tottery and feeble. He hobbled closer to Brand on foot, and peered at him as though he were a man studying mud that had dried on his boots and deciding how best to dislodge it.

Contemptuously, he slapped Brand's sword away. It clattered to the floor. Then he placed a hand upon Brand's head. The regent looked as though he was going to throw a punch, but the strength left his body. Instead, he collapsed to his knees once more.

"Yes, mortal," hissed the Rider. "Bow to me."

The regent could not stand, yet he lifted his head high and gazed at the Rider. There was determination in that gaze, and the will to succeed that had seen him survive countless fights. Yet his arms hung loose by his side and the only fight that he had left within him was in his eyes.

Gil reached out with his mind. He sensed Brand's heart flutter. It raced and thrummed unnaturally. He would die soon, and there was no Carnhaina here to save him this time. Gil could not bear it. He turned his mind toward the Rider, and he sensed the inevitability of time. It radiated from the figure in waves, but they were concentrated on Brand rather than the others in the room.

Even so, Gil felt the last dregs of his own strength drain from him. It slipped away like the wind stripping autumn leaves from a tree. Yet this magic was no spell. Not in the sense that Gil understood it. Instead, it stemmed from the very nature of the Rider, and its origin was from another world, and ever so faintly Gil sensed that the Rider was still connected to that world through the gateway that had been opened and through which he had been summoned.

He considered that. Each Rider was an embodiment of a great force, but the Riders were not really the things themselves. Brand, far more adept at lòhrengai than he, must have sensed these things also. But could that knowledge be turned to an advantage?

The Rider leaned in closer, placing both hands upon the regent's head now, and slowly they slid down Brand's face until the fingers, knobbed and deformed by arthritis, were at his temples. But the thumbs were near Brand's eyes, and they moved toward them.

"Beg, Brand of the Duthenor. Beg, Regent of Cardoroth. Beg, and perhaps I will spare your sight."

Brand gave no answer. But his eyes flashed with defiance.

Gil burned with fury. He sensed no weakness in the Rider, no way to exploit his understanding of where his power came from. But he would do anything to help. He prepared to act, to hurl his own power at the Rider, though he knew it would do no good.

The Rider pushed back Brand's head. His fingers stiffened and his thumbs went rigid as they pressed toward Brand's eyes.

Gil sensed the glee of the Rider, though it was lessened by Brand's defiance. He also felt the regent's fear. Above it all was a pall of horror that hung in the room thicker than smoke from the dying fire. His senses were alert, the lòhrengai within him ready to lash out and attack. It rose, furious like a wild animal that is caged but about to break free.

No! The command rang through Gil's mind. It was the strange girl, and her voice was as thunder in his head. *Not that way. Forget the Rider. Think of Brand!*

The lòhrengai in Gil roiled and seethed, trying to break free. He could not restrain it much longer, and that scared him. It was growing within him, and he was not sure he could control it.

He wanted to scream. If he could not unleash his lòhrengai upon the Rider, what then could he do? He tried to move forward to intervene physically, but he had not the strength to do so. The power of the Rider held him in place.

Now! yelled the girl within his mind. *Now!*

At last, Gil understood. He had not the skill with lòhrengai nor the strength of body to help Brand. But Brand had both. Gil had thought he would do anything for Brand, and so he would. But at last he knew what that should be.

He dismissed the Rider from his thoughts and focused only on the regent. He reached out to touch his mind. For a fleeting moment, for just a single instant in time, they became one. Their thoughts and memories merged. Above it all he felt the indomitable will of Brand, the determination of someone who would never give up. And in that moment he pulsed to him through their link the last of his own strength. It flowed from his body into Brand's. It flowed from his mind too. And lòhrengai went with it.

Gil fell forward to the floor. He tried to get back to his knees, but he had nothing left to give. Yet his eyes remained open, and he watched.

Brand reached out. Suddenly filled with strength, his arms snaked forward and caught hold of the Rider's head. The Rider released his own grip and tried to step back, sudden fear in his eyes, but Brand's grip was like iron. His hands twisted with a jerk. There was a sickening crack, and the Rider went limp. His head sagged loosely as Brand let him go and he fell to the tiled floors. Even as he hit the ground his horse screamed and reared up. But it too, joined by blood magic to the Rider, died. It fell writhing to the floor beside its master, and then lay still.

There was utter silence. A cold wind blew and green flame licked around the corpses. The stench of death filled the air, and Rider and mount disappeared in a waft of greasy smoke.

Once more, Gil tried to rise. But the world spun and darkness closed in. His heart fluttered rapidly, and then the great dark swallowed him.

29. I have Many Names

Brand ignored the Duthenor. He turned and ran to Gil. He knew what the boy had done for him, and what he had risked to give aid. He knew what the price of such a gift might be.

Gil lay there, unmoving. Brand reached down and felt for a pulse. It was there, but it was erratic and thready. Nor was his color good. He was pale, and a sheen of sweat glistened over his sickly skin.

All about him the Durlin and soldiers were moving. They had their swords drawn, and it appeared that the Duthenor were going to fight even though the odds were against them.

"Enough!" Brand said. He stood and pointed at the Duthenor. "Today, you have served a great evil. If you would repent that, put down your swords and wait on my justice."

The Duthenor looked uncertain. They knew they could die in the name of justice. They knew also that they *would* die if they fought. And beneath it all, there was undeniable truth in the statement that they had served evil.

One by one, they placed their swords on the tiled floor. Their leader was the last to do so, and he did not like it. He had the most to lose and the least expectation of leniency.

The men of Cardoroth surrounded them. Brand paid them no more heed. He knelt again beside Gil. Once more he felt for the boy's pulse. It was worse than before.

He felt a hand on his shoulder, its touch soft and gentle. A girl stood beside him, dressed in white. She was dazzlingly beautiful, but her eyes were sad.

He studied her a moment. That she had come with Gil he knew, but he did not know who she was. He knew that there was a strangeness about her though.

Elrika was there also. She knelt and took Gil's hands. There were tears in her eyes.

Brand looked back to the strange girl. Something about her disturbed him. She seemed in some way to be similar to the Riders, and yet he knew that she was not. "Who *are* you?"

She took her hand from his shoulder. "I have many names. I am light and shadow, day and night, heat and cold, love and hate." She paused for a moment, and then added. "Need I say more to one who has seen the heart of both good and evil?"

"No. You are balance. At least, that is your function here. You have been drawn into this world in the wake of the Riders. Nature always seeks harmony. But you, just like the Riders, aren't really here. Not yet, anyway. You are all shadows, the image of things drawn into this world while the reality remains in your own."

Her eyes widened slightly. "You are very perceptive. But the Riders would come to this world in truth, whereas I would not. And you can guess, therefore, how this must all end?"

Brand understood. She was connected to the Riders, and they to her, by the gateway through which they entered his world. They could not be separated. At least, not in Alithoras.

"Sadly, I do."

She looked upon him with wise eyes, and he felt the sorrow behind them. "But the boy does not. Nor should he. And there is balance in that … even as there was balance in you offering your life for his in the past and he doing the same for you just now."

"And yet I lived, and it seems that he will not."

"No, Brand. He will not die. Not this day, at least."

She knelt down beside him. Once more she rested her hand upon his shoulder, but now her other hand also touched Gil's face. She closed her eyes, and Brand marveled at her. He knew her fate should she succeed in her quest. The Riders must be returned to her world, and he knew now that there was only one way to do that. Not even death sufficed, for the gateway remained open and they could come through again. She was a creature of such sweetness, of such strength. But above it all was the determination to fulfill her purpose … no matter the cost.

He felt the warmth of her touch. He sensed her power. And then he perceived what she was doing. She was drawing back from him the strength that Gil had given.

The prince gasped. He rolled his head from side to side, and then his eyes flicked open. His gaze settled on Brand. A moment they looked at each other, and then Elrika had her arms about the boy, hugging him fiercely.

The lady beside him took her hands away from both of them, and straightened. Brand stood up beside her.

"Thank you, lady," he said.

She nodded gravely, but did not reply.

Brand turned to the Duthenor. Their weapons had been collected and placed in a pile on the floor. The men stood within a tight circle, the Durlin and the soldiers of Cardoroth surrounding them with drawn swords.

The leader gazed at Brand with a sullen expression.

"Let's get this over with."

Brand looked at him coolly. "Get what over with?"

"I'm in no mood to talk. Just kill us quickly."

Brand returned his look, ice cold hatred in exchange for sullenness. Then without speaking he walked across the tiled floor and retrieved his sword and helm. The Helm of the Duthenor he placed once more upon his head, but the sword he kept drawn. A little while he gazed at the leader of the group of traitors who served the usurper and who had also tried to assassinate Gil. If any men deserved death, it was these.

At length, he spoke. "You will not die. Not today. But you will leave the city, and never return. Should you do so, then surely your life will be forfeit."

The men looked at him. He could see that they did not believe it.

"Go!" he commanded. "Return to your master. Tell him this. His plot has failed. Tell him that I will soon return. And justice will come with me. He shall wish then that he were never born."

They looked at him, baffled by his lenience. "Go!" he commanded once more. "And take your swords with you."

This time, the Duthenor moved. They could not quite believe what was happening, and nor could Brand's own men. Yet the Camar allowed them through to their weapons.

The Duthenor retrieved their blades from the floor, but the leader hesitated.

"Pick it up," Brand said. "But don't even think of using it."

The man reached for his blade. A moment he held it, and then he slammed it home in its sheath. His men sheathed theirs also.

"One last thing," Brand said. "I am the rightful chieftain of the Duthenor. You serve a usurper. But think well on this. You serve a traitor. It will not end well for you. He is doomed, and so will you be, while you serve him. This grace to depart in freedom that I have now given you is done as Regent of Cardoroth. Should I need to judge you one day as Chieftain of the Duthenor, I will be harsher."

The leader looked at him. "You seek to turn us to your cause?"

Brand shook his head. "No. You would need to change greatly before I would have you serve me. You are not good men. Yet neither are you truly evil. Go home. Pass on my message. Then, you shall stand at a crossroads. Serve the usurper and die. Leave him, and your destiny will be far richer."

The leader stared at Brand. "I knew you of old, though you don't remember me. You were never a prophet. Nor a seer. These are just words."

"I was never Regent of Cardoroth before," Brand replied. "Nor a lòhren. Now I am both. I have grown, and so may yet you. And I *do* remember you. Your name is Rathbold. Once upon a time you were apprenticed to the village blacksmith. But he dismissed you and you took up a life of outlawry in the forest."

The leader was surprised by this, but he said nothing. Instead, he gave a single curt nod and led his men from the courtyard.

Shorty came over to Brand as the Duthenor filed out. "They'll not change," he said.

178

The strange girl heard his words. Her gaze had been on the Duthenor as they left, but she had been watching them as though she saw with a sight beyond that of eyes.

"No, they will not," she agreed. "But one will, and he will do great good in the world that otherwise would not have happened." She curtsied to Brand as she spoke.

Shorty gave her a careful look, unsure who she was or what she was doing there but recognizing that Brand knew these things.

"But still," he continued. "To see them just walk out of here after what they've done. That's not right."

"No," Brand agreed. "It isn't. But it will send word swifter than an arrow to my people that I'm coming home. That word will spread wherever those men go. The rumor will catch like wildfire. And the usurper will begin to know fear. In the end, the release of these men will help topple a cruel tyrant. So, although justice is not served in Cardoroth, it will have a better chance of prospering in the lands of the Duthenor."

Shorty thought about that. Then he shook his head. "You always look at the bigger picture. But for myself, I would have killed them. Anyway, how do you know they'll not find another hideout in Cardoroth and keep plotting against you?"

Brand shrugged. "They might do that. But if I'm any judge of men, especially Duthenor men, they won't. They know that to stay is to die, and they would rather live."

"Brand is right," the strange girl said. "And also, the leader has lost the confidence of his men. He might have wished to stay, but the men have had enough."

Shorty looked at her again, his expression curious. "It is a pleasure to meet you, lady. But who are you?"

179

She smiled at him. "A friend, Lornach. But if I need a name, then please call me … call me Lady. I like that."

Shorty bowed. "Then, the White Lady you are."

There was a commotion nearby. Despite Elrika's protests, Gil had stood up. His legs seemed wobbly, and his skin was pale. But there was a smile on his face.

"We did it," he said.

"That we did," Brand answered. Then he hugged him. They separated and looked at each other. "You've grown, Gil. You're ready to come into your own."

"Let's not talk about that just yet. Today is a day for celebration. We've defeated a Rider. At least you have, with a little help. And there are only two more to go before it's all over."

Brand looked at the White Lady, and he saw the truth in her eyes.

"It is not that simple," she said to Gil. "Two Riders are defeated. But they may yet come again, for the gateway remains open. And there are two left undefeated, Betrayal and War. Nor is that all. War is not just a name, but also his function. Even as we speak an army gathers against you, and War shall lead it."

Gil let out a sigh. "An army? And it's ready to march upon us?"

"Verily," the White Lady answered.

Gil turned to Brand. "You're still regent, assuming that you want to remain so. What do you suggest we do?"

"I have something yet to offer Cardoroth," Brand answered. "My day of departure is coming, but it won't be for a little while yet. I suggest two things. You must close the gateway, and I must prepare a strategy to defeat the army that comes against us. But I suspect, Gil, that the two are linked. Neither the gateway will be closed nor the enemy defeated until a great battle has been fought."

The White Lady nodded, but did not offer any information. Brand knew there was much she could say though. Yet perhaps she was right. Some things were better off unknown until the end.

He looked back at Gil. The boy that he once had tutored was gone. A young man now stood before him.

"One last thing, Gil. You will be king one day very soon. Though I remain regent for a while longer, the truth is that you now command. At least, I shall defer to your will should we disagree."

Gil heard those words, and even as he did so Brand saw the weight of responsibility settle over his shoulders. It was a weight that could crush. He hoped the prince was strong enough to bear it. For all that had happened so far was but a shadow of what was yet to come. And it was coming soon.

Thus ends *Sword of the Blood.* The Son of Sorcery series will continue in *Light of the Realm*, where Gil will face the gathering threat to Cardoroth and attempt to fulfil the quest bestowed upon him.

Sign up below and be the first to hear about new book releases, see previews and learn of upcoming discounts. http://eepurl.com/Rswv1

Visit my website at www.homeofhighfantasy.com

Dedication

There's a growing movement in fantasy literature. Its name is noblebright, and it's the opposite of grimdark.

Noblebright celebrates the virtues of heroism. It's an old-fashioned thing, as old as the first story ever told around a smoky campfire beneath ancient stars. It's storytelling that highlights courage and loyalty and hope for the spirit of humanity. It recognizes the dark, the dark in us all, and the dark in the villains of its stories. It recognizes death, and treachery and betrayal. But it dwells on none of those things.

I dedicate this book, such as it is, to that which is noblebright. And I thank the authors before me who held the torch high so that I could see the path: J.R.R. Tolkien, C.S. Lewis, Terry Brooks, David Eddings, Susan Cooper, Roger Taylor and many others. I salute you.

And, for a time, I too will hold the torch as high as I can.

Encyclopedic Glossary

Note: the glossary of each book in this series is individualized for that book alone. Additionally, there is often historical material provided in its entries for people, artifacts and events that are not included in the main text.

Many races dwell in Alithoras. All have their own language, and though sometimes related to one another, the changes sparked by migration, isolation and various influences often render these tongues unintelligible to each other.

The ascendancy of Halathrin culture, combined with their widespread efforts to secure and maintain allies against elug incursions, has made their language the primary means of communication between diverse peoples.

For instance, a soldier of Cardoroth addressing a ship's captain from Camarelon would speak Halathrin, or a simplified version of it, even though their native speeches stem from the same ancestral language.

This glossary contains a range of names and terms. Many are of Halathrin origin, and their meaning is provided. The remainder derive from native tongues and are obscure, so meanings are only given intermittently.

Often, Camar names and Halathrin elements are combined. This is especially so for the aristocracy. No other tribes of men had such long-term friendship with the immortal Halathrin, and though in this relationship they lost some of their natural culture, they gained nobility and knowledge in return.

List of abbreviations:

Azn. Azan

Cam. Camar

Comb. Combined

Cor. Corrupted form

Duth. Duthenor

Hal. Halathrin

Leth. Letharn

Prn. Pronounced

Age of Heroes: A period of Camar history that has become mythical. Many tales are told of this time. Some are true while others are not. Yet, even the false ones usually contain elements of historical fact. Many were the heroes who walked abroad during this time, and they are remembered and honored still by the Camar people. The old days are looked back on with pride, and the descendants of many heroes walk the streets of Cardoroth unaware of their heritage and the accomplishments of their forefathers.

Alithoras: *Hal.* "Silver land." The Halathrin name for the continent they settled after their exodus from their homeland. Refers to the extensive river and lake systems they found and their wonder at the beauty of the land.

Anast Dennath: *Hal.* "Stone mountains." Mountain range in northern Alithoras. Source of the river known as the Careth Nien that forms a natural barrier between the lands of the Camar people and the Duthenor and related tribes.

Arach Neben: *Hal.* "West gate." The defensive wall surrounding Cardoroth has four gates. Each is named after a cardinal direction, and each carries a token to represent a celestial object. Arach Neben bears a steel ornament of the Morning Star.

Aranloth: *Hal.* "Noble might." A lòhren. Founder and head of the lòhren order. A great friend of Gilcarist's grandparents.

Arell: Rumored to be Brand's lover. A name formerly common among the Camar people, but nowadays out of favor in Cardoroth. Its etymology is obscure, though it is speculated that it derives from the Halathrin stems "aran" and "ell" meaning noble and slender. Ell, in the Halathrin tongue, also refers to any type of timber that is pliable, for instance, hazel. This is cognate with our word wych-wood, meaning timber that is supple and pliable. As elùgroths use wych-wood staffs as instruments of sorcery, it is sometimes supposed their name derives from this stem, rather than elù (shadowed). This is a plausible philological theory. Nevertheless, as a matter of historical fact, it is wrong.

Aurellin: *Cor. Hal.* The first element means blue. The second is native Camar. Formerly Queen of Cardoroth, wife to Gilhain and grandmother to Gilcarist.

Betrayal: One of the Riders, also called Horsemen, summoned into Alithoras by Ginsar. He represents and instigates betrayal. Yet, in truth, the Riders are spirit-beings from another world. They have been given form and nature within Alithoras by Ginsar. The form provided by her is part of the blood sorcery that binds them to her will. In their own world, they do not bear these names or natures. Yet they are creatures wholly of evil, and though bound by Ginsar they seek to break that bond. Even if defeated, the bond from the summoning persists and the Riders are capable of rising again, even though they are considered dead.

Brand: A Duthenor tribesman. Appointed by the former king of Cardoroth to serve as regent for Gilcarist. By birth, he is the rightful chieftain of the Duthenor people. However, a usurper overthrew his father, killing both him and his wife. Brand, only a youth at the time, swore an oath of vengeance. That oath sleeps, but it is not forgotten, either by Brand or the usurper.

Camar: *Cam. Prn.* Kay-mar. A race of interrelated tribes that migrated in two main stages. The first brought them to the vicinity of Halathar, homeland of the immortal Halathrin; in the second, they separated and established cities along a broad stretch of eastern Alithoras.

Cardoroth: *Cor. Hal. Comb. Cam.* A Camar city, often called Red Cardoroth. Some say this alludes to the red granite commonly used in the construction of its buildings, others that it refers to a prophecy of destruction.

Cardurleth: *Hal.* "Car – red, dur – steadfast, leth – stone." The defensive wall that surrounds Cardoroth. Established soon after the city's founding and constructed of red granite. It looks displeasing to the eye, but the people of the city love it nonetheless. They believe it impregnable and hold that no enemy shall ever breach it – except by treachery.

Careth Nien: *Hal. Prn.* Kareth nyen. "Great river." Largest river in Alithoras. Has its source in the mountains of Anast Dennath and runs southeast across the land before emptying into the sea. It was over this river (which sometimes freezes along its northern stretches) that the Camar and other tribes migrated into the eastern lands. Much later, Brand came to the city of Cardoroth by one of these ancient migratory routes.

Carnhaina: First element native *Cam.* Second *Hal.* "Heroine." An ancient queen of Cardoroth. Revered as a savior of her people, but to some degree also feared for she possessed powers of magic. Hated to this day by elùgroths because she overthrew their power unexpectedly at a time when their dark influence was rising. According to legend, kept alive mostly within the royal family of Cardoroth, she guards the city even in death and will return in its darkest hour.

Chapterhouse: Special halls set aside in the palace of Cardoroth for the private meetings, teachings and military training of the Durlin.

Death: One of the Riders, also called Horsemen, summoned into Alithoras by Ginsar. He represents and instigates Death. Yet, in truth, the Riders are spirit-beings from another world. They have been given form and nature within Alithoras by Ginsar. The form provided by her is part of the blood sorcery that binds them to her will. In their own world, they do not bear these names or natures. Yet they are creatures wholly of evil, and though bound by Ginsar they seek to break that bond. Even if defeated, the bond from the summoning persists and the Riders are capable of rising again, even though they are considered dead.

Dernbrael: *Hal.* "Sharp tongued." By some translations, "cunning tongued." A lord of Cardoroth. Out of favor with the old king due to mistrust. Attempted to usurp the throne from Gilcarist, and now in hiding after his scheme failed. It is said that he is in league with the traitor Hvargil, though this has never been proven. It is known, however, that Hvargil once saved his life when they were younger men. This occurred in a gambling den of ill-repute, and the details are obscure. Nevertheless, all accounts agree that Hvargil was wounded protecting his friend.

Drinbar: A captain in Cardoroth's army. Loyal to Brand and Gil. His father was once a Durlin who guarded King Gilhain.

Durlin: *Hal.* "The steadfast." The original Durlin were the seven sons of the first king of Cardoroth. They guarded him against all enemies, of which there were many, and three died to protect him. Their tradition continued throughout Cardoroth's history, suspended only once, and briefly, some four hundred years ago when it was discovered that three members were secretly in the service of elùgroths. These were imprisoned, but committed suicide while waiting for the king's trial to commence. It is rumored that the king himself provided them with the knives that they used. It is said that he felt sorry for them and gave them this way out to avoid the shame a trial would bring to their families.

Durlin creed: These are the native Camar words, long remembered and greatly honored, that were uttered by the first Durlin to die while he defended his father, who was also the king, from attack. Tum del conar – El dar tum! Death or infamy – I choose death!

Durlindrath: *Hal.* "Lord of the steadfast." The title given to the leader of the Durlin. For the first time in the history of Cardoroth, that position is held jointly by two people: Lornach and Taingern. Lornach also possesses the title of King's Champion. The latter honor is not held in quite such high esteem, yet it carries somewhat more power. As King's Champion, Lornach is authorized to act in the king's stead in matters of honor and treachery to the Crown.

Duthenor: *Duth. Prn.* Dooth-en-or. "The people." A single tribe, or sometimes a group of closely related tribes melded into a larger people at times of war or disaster, who generally live a rustic and peaceful lifestyle. They are breeders of cattle and herders of sheep. However, when need demands they are bold warriors – men and women alike. Currently ruled by a usurper who murdered Brand's parents. Brand has sworn an oath to overthrow the tyrant and avenge his parents.

Elrika: *Cam.* Daughter of the royal baker. Friend to Gilcarist, and greatly skilled in weapons fighting, especially the long sword. Brand has given instructions to Lornach that she is to be taught all arts of the warrior to the full extent of her ability. He is grooming her to be the first female Durlin in the history of the city.

Elùgrune: *Hal.* Literally "shadowed fortune," but is also translated into "ill fortune" and "born of the dark." In the first two senses it means bad luck. In the third, it connotes a person steeped in shadow and mystery and not to be trusted. In some circles, the term has an additional meaning of "mystic".

Elugs: *Hal.* "That which creeps in shadows." An evil and superstitious race that dwells in the south of Alithoras, especially the Graèglin Dennath Mountains. They also inhabit portions of the northern mountains of Alithoras, and have traditionally fallen under the sway of elùgroths centered in the region of Cardoroth.

Elùdrath: *Hal. Prn.* Eloo-drath. "Shadowed lord." A sorcerer. First and greatest among elùgroths. Believed by most to be dead, but rumored by some to yet live.

Elùgai: *Hal. Prn.* Eloo-guy. "Shadowed force." The sorcery of an elùgroth.

Elùgroth: *Hal. Prn.* Eloo-groth. "Shadowed horror." A sorcerer. They often take names in the Halathrin tongue in mockery of the lòhren practice to do so.

Esanda: No known etymology for this name. Likewise, Esanda herself is not native to Cardoroth. King Gilhain believed she was from the city of Esgallien, but he was not certain of this. Esanda refuses to answer questions concerning her origins. Regardless of the personal mystery attached to her, she was one of Gilhain's most trusted advisors and soon became so to Brand. She leads a ring of spies utterly devoted to the protection of Cardoroth from the many dark forces that would bring it down.

Esgallien: *Hal. Prn.* Ez-gally-en. "Es – rushing water, gal(en) – green, lien – to cross: place of the crossing onto the green plains." A city founded in antiquity and named after a nearby ford of the Careth Nien. Reports indicate it has fallen to elugs.

Felargin: *Cam.* A sorcerer, and brother to Ginsar. Acolyte of Shurilgar the elùgroth. Steeped in evil and once lured Brand, Lornach and other adventurers under false pretenses into a quest. Only Brand and Shorty survived the betrayal. Felargin, however, fell victim to the trap he had prepared for the others. Brand was responsible for his death.

Foresight: Premonition of the future. Can occur at random but is also deliberately sought by entering the shadow world between life and death where the spirit is released from the body to travel through space and time. To achieve this, the body must be brought to the threshold of death. The first method is uncontrollable and rare. The second exceedingly rare but somewhat controllable for those with the skill and the courage, or the desperate need, to risk the danger.

Forgotten Queen (the): An epithet of Queen Carnhaina. She was a person of immense power and presence, yet she made few friends in life, and her possession of magic caused her to be mistrusted. For these reasons, memory of her accomplishments faded soon after her passing and only small remnants of her rule are remembered by the populace of Cardoroth.

Gil: See Gilcarist.

Gilcarist: *Comb. Cam & Hal.* First element unknown, second "ice." Heir to the throne of Cardoroth and grandson of King Gilhain. According to Carnhaina, his coming was told in the stars. He is also foretold by her as The Savior and The Destroyer. The prophecies mean little to him, for he believes in Brand's view that a man makes his own fate.

Gilhain: *Comb. Cam & Hal.* First element unknown, second "hero." King of Cardoroth before proclaiming Brand regent for Gilcarist, the underage heir to the throne. Husband to Aurellin.

Ginsar: *Cam.* A sorceress. Sister to Felargin. Acolyte of Shurilgar the elùgroth. Steeped in evil and greatly skilled in the arts of elùgai, reaching a level of proficiency nearly as great as her master. Rumored to be insane.

Goblins: See elugs.

Gorfalac: Cam. "Sword of the realm." An epithet for king. It literally signifies *sword of the blood*, and was a term in much use during the ancient days when the Camar migrated and danger surrounded them. The king was seen as protector of the people, and his courage and willingness to fight for them was his inherited duty.

Graèglin Dennath: *Hal. Prn.* Greg-lin dennath. "Mountains of ash." Chain of mountains in southern

193

Alithoras. The landscape is one of jagged stone and boulder, relieved only by gaping fissures from which plumes of ashen smoke ascend, thus leading to its name. Believed to be impassable because of the danger of poisonous air flowing from cracks, and the ground unexpectedly giving way, swallowing any who dare to tread its forbidden paths. In other places swathes of molten stone run in rivers down its slopes.

Grindar: *Cam.* A lamplighter in Cardoroth. Once a soldier serving Gilcarist's great grandfather.

Halathar: *Hal.* "Dwelling place of the people of Halath." The forest realm of the immortal Halathrin.

Halathgar: *Hal.* "Bright star." Actually a constellation of two stars. Also called the Lost Huntress.

Halathrin: *Hal.* "People of Halath." A race named after an honored lord who led an exodus of his people to the land of Alithoras in pursuit of justice, having sworn to defeat a great evil. They are human, though of fairer form, greater skill and higher culture than ordinary men. They possess a unity of body, mind and spirit that enables insight and endurance beyond the native races of Alithoras. Said to be immortal, but killed in great numbers during their conflicts in ancient times with the evil they sought to destroy. Those conflicts are collectively known as the Shadowed Wars.

Harath Neben: *Hal.* "North gate." This gate bears a token of two massive emeralds representing the constellation of Halathgar. The gate is also called "Hunter's Gate," for the north road out of the city leads to wild lands of plentiful game.

Hruilgar: *Comb. Cam & Hal.* First element unknown (but thought to mean "wild"), second "star." The old king's huntsman. Rumored to have learned his craft as a tracker in Esgallien and to have journeyed north to Cardoroth at the same time as Esanda.

Hvargil: Prince of Cardoroth. Younger son of Carangil, former king of Cardoroth. Exiled by Carangil for treason after it was discovered he plotted with elùgroths to assassinate his older half-brother, Gilhain, and prevent him from ascending the throne. He gathered a band about him in exile of outlaws and discontents. Most came from Cardoroth but others were drawn from the southern Camar cities. He fought with the invading army of elugs against Cardoroth in the previous war.

Immortals: See Halathrin.

Lake Alithorin: *Hal.* "Silver lake." A mysterious lake of northern Alithoras.

Letharn: *Hal.* "Stone Raisers. Builders." A race of people that in antiquity conquered most of Alithoras. Now, only faint traces of their civilization endure.

Lòhren: *Hal. Prn.* Ler-ren. "Knowledge giver – a counselor." Other terms used by various nations include wizard, druid and sage.

Lòhren-fire: A combat manifestation of lòhrengai. The color of flame varies according to the temperament of the lòhren.

Lòhrengai: *Hal. Prn.* Ler-ren-guy. "Lòhren force." Enchantment, spell or use of mystic power. A manipulation and transformation of the natural energy

195

inherent in all things. Each use takes something from the user. Likewise, some part of the transformed energy infuses them. Lòhrens use it sparingly, elùgroths indiscriminately.

Lòrenta: *Hal. Prn.* Ler-rent-a. "Hills of knowledge." Uplands in northern Alithoras where the stronghold of the lòhrens is established. It is to here that the old king and queen of Cardoroth traveled to spend their remaining years.

Lornach: *Cam.* A former Durlin and now joint Durlindrath. Also holds the title of King's Champion. Friend to Brand, and often called by his nickname of "Shorty."

Lost Huntress: See Halathgar.

Magic: Mystic power. See lòhrengai and elùgai.

Merril: *Cam.* Wife to Thrimgern the blacksmith. A popular name in Cardoroth. Once considered a man's name, but used by a female archer of outstanding skill some two hundred years ago who achieved fame by surviving a skirmish with elugs north of the city while hunting and consequently has become a common female name.

Mother of Stars: A term of obscure origin, often used in mystic societies. It has various interpretations, but the most commonly accepted is that it signifies "the universe".

Nightborn: See elùgrune.

Otherworld: Camar term for a mingling of half-remembered history, myth and the spirit world. Sometimes used interchangeably with the term "Age of Heroes."

Parviel: *Cam.* A Durlin. Slain by Duthenor conspirators while guarding Gilcarist. Said to have been the best knife fighter among the Durlin.

Rathbold: *Duth.* A former outlaw in the lands of the Duthenor. He offered his service to the usurper, and was pardoned. He rose to prominence in the usurper's eyes due to his complete lack of scruples and his willingness to carry out any task. Eventually, became one of his most trusted advisors.

Rhodeurl: *Cam.* A Durlin. Slain by Duthenor conspirators while guarding Gilcarist. Said to have descended from a noble family who emigrated from the southern Camar cities to Cardoroth. The "rhod" element of his name is common in the south but not in Cardoroth. A man of great wealth who put it aside to pursue the skills of a Durlin.

Sandy: See Esanda.

Seal of Halathgar: A representation of the Constellation of Halathgar. Also known as the Seal of Carnhaina, for the Great Queen took it as her personal emblem.

Sellic Neben: *Hal.* "East gate." This gate bears a representation, crafted of silver and pearl, of the moon rising over the sea.

Shadowed Lord: See Elùdrath.

Shorty: See Lornach.

Shurilgar: *Hal.* "Midnight star." An elùgroth. One of the most puissant sorcerers of antiquity. Known to legend as the Betrayer of Nations.

Sight: The ability to discern the intentions or thoughts of another person. Not reliable, and yet effective at times.

Sorcerer: See Elùgroth.

Sorcery: See elùgai.

Stele: A vertical stone slab engraved with inscriptions or symbols. Used by most cultures in Alithoras. Sometimes constructed of wood, but these do not generally endure.

Surcoat: An outer garment usually worn over chainmail. The Durlin surcoat is unadorned white, which is a tradition carried down from the order's inception.

Sword and Crown Tavern: A tavern in Cardoroth. Owned by Esanda and used by her as a safe-house to hide discovered informants and to gather intelligence. Frequented by high-ranking military officers and nobles. Their conversations are often heard by the barmaids, who are skilled operatives reporting to Esanda.

Taingern: *Cam.* A former Durlin. Friend to Brand, and now joint Durlindrath. Once, in company of Brand, saved the tomb of Carnhaina from defilement and robbery by an elùgroth.

Thrimgern: A blacksmith of high skill.

Time: One of the Riders, also called Horsemen, summoned into Alithoras by Ginsar. He represents

Time – specifically as manifested by the aging process. Yet, in truth, the Riders are spirit-beings from another world. They have been given form and nature within Alithoras by Ginsar. The form provided by her is part of the blood sorcery that binds them to her will. In their own world, they do not bear these names or natures. Yet they are creatures wholly of evil, and though bound by Ginsar they seek to break that bond. Even if defeated, the bond from the summoning persists and the Riders are capable of rising again, even though they are considered dead.

Tower of Halathgar: In life, a place of study of Queen Carnhaina. In death, her resting place. Unusually, her sarcophagus rests on the tower's parapet beneath the stars.

Unlach Neben: *Hal.* "South gate." This gate bears a representation of the sun, crafted of gold, beating down upon an arid land. Said to signify the southern homeland of the elugs, whence the gold of the sun was obtained by an adventurer of old.

Ùhrengai: *Hal. Prm.* Er-ren-guy. "Original force." The primordial force that existed before substance or time.

War: One of the Riders, also called Horsemen, summoned into Alithoras by Ginsar. He represents conflict and battle. Yet, in truth, the Riders are spirit-beings from another world. They have been given form and nature within Alithoras by Ginsar. The form provided by her is part of the blood sorcery that binds them to her will. In their own world, they do not bear these names or natures. Yet they are creatures wholly of evil, and though bound by Ginsar they seek to break that bond. Even if defeated, the bond from the summoning persists and the Riders are capable of rising again, even though they are considered dead.

White Lady: A being of spirit drawn into Alithoras as an unintended consequence of Ginsar's summoning of the Riders.

Witch Queen: See Carnhaina

Wizard: See lòhren.

Wych-wood: A general description for a range of supple and springy timbers. Some hardy varieties are prevalent on the poisonous slopes of the Graèglin Dennath Mountains, and are favored by elùgroths as instruments of sorcery.

About the author

I'm a man born in the wrong era. My heart yearns for faraway places and even further afield times. Tolkien had me at the beginning of *The Hobbit* when he said, ". . . one morning long ago in the quiet of the world . . ."

Sometimes I imagine myself in a Viking mead-hall. The long winter night presses in, but the shimmering embers of a log in the hearth hold back both cold and dark. The chieftain calls for a story, and I take a sip from my drinking horn and stand up . . .

Or maybe the desert stars shine bright and clear, obscured occasionally by wisps of smoke from burning camel dung. A dry gust of wind marches sand grains across our lonely campsite, and the wayfarers about me stir restlessly. I sip cool water and begin to speak.

I'm a storyteller. A man to paint a picture by the slow music of words. I like to bring faraway places and times to life, to make hearts yearn for something they can never have, unless for a passing moment.

36809178R00118

Printed in Great Britain
by Amazon